Wyon...

Mary Langer Smith

ACCENT BOOKS
Denver, Colorado

ACCENT BOOKS

A division of Accent Publications, Inc.
12100 West Sixth Avenue
P.O. Box 15337
Denver, Colorado 80215

Library of Congress Catalog Card Number 86-70150

ISBN 0-89636-211-6

Dedication

*To all my family
for their love and support*

Chapter 1

Standing at the clothesline behind the hotel she had inherited upon the death of her parents, Carrie Benson looked up from pinning the last sheet. Nervous, her eyes made another sweeping study of the wide basin that stretched on every side of tiny Parke's Crossing, Wyoming.

Lately, she'd felt that Parke's Crossing was too near the Indian reservation and too far from the nearest military post. Rumor had it the young Shoshone bucks, full of wild talk, were growing bolder in their forays off the reservation. Today, the Indian smoke-talk silhouetted against the brassy summer sky filled Carrie with dread. Peering across the tall grasses moving in green-gold waves before the August wind, Carrie imagined Indians, hidden in that grassy sea, crawling toward her. She gripped the clothesline until her knuckles whitened under the tanned skin.

In the shimmering noonday heat, the blacksmith's anvil in the livery stable across the street from her hotel stood silent. In its place, a rasping chorus of locusts came from the cottonwoods that lined the creek. Carrie bent to retrieve her clothes basket, letting her eyes trail to the west. Her gaze followed the willow-lined path of the meandering stream which ran down from the mountains in a deep gully before widening into the ford in front of her.

A movement in the distance captured her attention. Rigid, straining to see, she watched a solitary horseman riding slowly toward Parke's Crossing and Carrie. He was scarcely visible as he blended into the purple background of distant, needle-peaked mountains.

Indians! She bit back a cry. Struggling to contain the fear which hammered against her chest like tom-toms, Carrie withdrew to the rear wall of the hotel. Camouflaged by a thin line of shade, she forced herself to wait until she could be sure. There would still be time to sound the alarm. She ran trembling fingers over the damp wisps of hair along the nape of her neck and held her breath.

As the lone figure drew steadily nearer, Carrie could tell he wasn't an Indian. Her breathing returned to normal. The screeching locust song lessened as the stranger approached, then ceased entirely when the rider and his dusty, lathered horse arrived at the ford. The animal splashed into the stream and began drinking in loud, thirsty gulps.

Even slumped over in the saddle as he was, Carrie saw that the stranger was a tall man. A war bag and canteen hung behind the saddle and a rifle rested in its scabbard within easy reach of his right hand. Sweat darkened the sun-faded blue calico shirt, and gloved hands clutched the reins and saddle horn. A maroon blotch had spread over one leg of his butternut-colored trousers. Even from this distance, Carrie could see blood drip, drop by slow drop, off the stirrup and into the hock-high water.

Her fear gone, Carrie raced across the rocky flat and waded into the creek. When she gently pulled the reins from the wounded man's hands, he roused slightly and raised a haggard face, flushed and salt-streaked from perspiration. Blue-black eyes, sunken and bright with fever, caught and held Carrie's eyes.

Please, dear Lord, let me be in time to help him, she prayed earnestly, watching him sag lower in the saddle.

"What're you doing?" he murmured.

"Just hold tight. I'm leading your horse," she said.

"Where to?" He shook his head slightly and squinted as though trying to bring her into focus.

She motioned toward the weathered log hotel which dominated the single dusty street. "To food and a bed. It's not far."

His head sank again. "It better not be," he said so weakly she nearly missed it.

Carrie led the horse past the few cabins where people stood looking cautiously from doorways, until she came abreast of her hotel and Hardesty's Trading Post which was directly across from it.

She stopped in the middle of the street and looked over at Parke's Crossing's self-styled first citizen. Phil Hardesty lounged easily against the log wall of his Post, the sole of one boot planted firmly on the second log, the other thick leg propping him up.

Of average height and wide both across and through, he was dressed in well-worn but clean range clothes. Despite his over forty years, his full, weathered face was remarkably unlined. A bristly, dark mustache filled his upper lip and, below the rim of his sweat-stained Stetson, thick salt-and-pepper hair curled above his ears. Heavy eyebrows, blacker than his dark eyes, joined above the bridge of his short, flat nose.

Phil had been operating his trading business out of a tent when the Bensons had first arrived in 1865, ten years ago. They had seen the need for a hotel and stayed to build one. Parke's Crossing, halfway to the Montana Territory border, had continued to grow on the banks of the ford. It was a place for tired travelers to stop for the night and replenish their supplies before continuing north to the gold fields in Montana.

"Phil!" Carrie called. "Give me a hand, please."

He made no move to join her.

Carrie found herself irritated over his perpetual reluctance to become involved in anything that didn't net him a profit.

"A stranger just rode in from the west," she said, unable to keep her vexation at Phil from her voice. "He's run into some trouble."

Phil hesitated still, as though weighing her words.

She let her eyes run over the small crowd of children, tired women, and feeble elderly. "I can't lift him alone," she snapped. "Help me!"

After taking several moments to contemplate her order, Phil pushed away from the wall and lazily moved to the edge of the trading post veranda. Looking at Carrie rather than at the sagging figure, he asked, "What're you planning to do?"

Sunk in pain, the wounded man shifted in the saddle, weaving slightly. Carrie laid a steadying hand on his arm as she forced herself to return a civil reply to Phil's question. Phil would be pushed only so far before he balked, and right now she needed his help. "I plan on getting him off this horse and into a bed. Then clean up

8

the wound and feed him."

Phil nodded and stepped off the veranda. Small clouds of dust spun up and settled over his scuffed, mid-calf boots as he walked to meet her in the center of the wide street separating their two establishments.

Carrie handed him the reins. "Bring his horse along while I spread up a bed," she said. "We'll never get him upstairs. Let's put him in the wash house."

Some of the more curious townspeople gathered to watch the wounded stranger being carried into the small building behind Carrie's hotel.

"Smart to bed him here," Phil said in his rasping voice as they laid him on an old mattress. "No use tying up a good room when like as not you won't see a penny for your trouble."

Carrie glared at him from where she knelt, cutting the pant leg away from the wound. "I put him in the wash house so I can keep closer track of him than if he were upstairs. He'll be near to plenty of hot water and only a few steps from the kitchen."

Dismissing Phil with a curt nod, she rose and filled a basin with hot water from the boiler on the little jack stove in the center of the room. Without looking at Phil again, Carrie returned to the bedside and started washing the ragged wound.

Staring for a moment, Phil finally shrugged his disinterest, turned, and shoved his way through the curious onlookers filling the doorway as he left.

"Elsa!" Carrie called.

A tall, angular woman of, perhaps, thirty-five stepped into the room. She stopped at Carrie's elbow. Her pale blue eyes were glued to the inert form on the bed, and her long face was expressionless as she awaited instructions.

Carrie looked up and smiled. "Please build up the fire

and set more water to heat. I'll need gallons. Then find an old sheet we can tear for bandages."

"Sure, Carrie," Elsa said, seeming relieved that she hadn't been asked to help dress the wound. She wiped her hands on an apron that showed hard use and pushed her way back through the crowd blocking the doorway.

It irritated Carrie that her neighbors stood and gawked at the helpless man. "Any of you folks who care to help, step right on in," she said over her shoulder.

As if by magic, the entrance became vacant. She smiled and gave thanks for the faint movement of air which now flowed in through the empty doorway, cooling her slightly as she worked on the gaping wound.

The stranger opened confused, fever-filled eyes and cast a wary glance at his surroundings. Just then Carrie applied pressure to the wound to stop the bleeding. He winced and closed his eyes, leaving her unobserved to study the weather-burnished face noticeably shadowed with reddish beard stubble. She wondered if the square jaw indicated a stubborn nature and decided she would undoubtedly know before he was able to leave. Above the wide mouth, pulled narrow against pain, bristled a carefully trimmed chestnut-colored mustache. Jutting cheekbones accented the deeply recessed eyes. His nose, probably once well-formed, appeared to have been altered by unpleasant circumstances and now had an obvious curve.

Carrie removed the pressure and noted that the wound remained clear. Carefully she washed the torn edges. He winced again. "I'm sorry I'm hurting you," she said softly.

"Do what you must." His voice was weak, the words slurred.

"The bleeding's stopped. But I'm going to put on some

liniment that's going to sting like fury." Carrie felt it only fair to warn him. "Then I'll bandage your leg."

She carefully poured the liniment into the open wound. His body went instantly rigid and the muscles of his jaws twitched, acknowledgment of the fire the liquid had created in his leg. Maybe, Carrie thought, if she continued to talk it would draw his mind from the pain. "By the way, I haven't seen you in these parts. Mind telling me your name?" she asked.

His eyes squinted open the tiniest bit and he cleared his throat. "King. Dan King. Yours?" His voice came out a breathless, nearly inaudible whisper.

"Carrie Benson." Then, pausing to decide how much she wanted to tell him, she added, "I own the hotel."

"Hmmm," he murmured, closing his eyes again.

By the time Carrie finished dressing the wound, his rhythmic breathing told her that Dan King slept. *Thank you, Lord, for being here and giving me the help I needed,* she prayed. With a single backward glance, Carrie left to return to her duties in the hotel.

Only a few stingy rays from the oil lamp burning low on the cold stove greeted Dan when he roused again. Though the glass chimney was well-cleaned, he could see only a few feet. He wondered what time it was and where he was. The place didn't look familiar. Forlornly, he thought, *Where am I, Lord?*

A rumble deep inside brought an awareness that he was ravenously hungry. His fever seemed gone, but his mouth held thick, cotton-feeling remnants and his leg still throbbed. Only patches of the day's events were clear: a sandy-haired woman with gentle hands had bandaged his leg after pouring something on it that burned viciously; and a heavy-set older man had talked with her briefly. His

11

rough voice nagged at Dan. He'd heard it before but as he tried to remember where, the time and place kept evading him. It had been in extremely unpleasant circumstances he was sure.

Dan pulled a worn leather billfold from the buckskin jacket beside him. His fumbling fingers removed a battered daguerreotype of a beautiful young woman standing before a white-columned house with cypress trees dripping moss. He studied the smiling face. A mighty pretty woman, his Anna. He sighed and wondered what his life would have been like if she and the baby hadn't died. But remembering only strengthened his resolution never to bring a woman into this wilderness again. There was so little for a lady. This Territory had broken his Anna and she had died from it.

Returning the picture to its protected slot, he extracted his money and counted it. He didn't carry much, but what he had was intact.

He couldn't say as much for his leg, but he guessed he shouldn't complain. Yesterday, just when he thought he had picked up the trail of his rustled cattle, something had spooked his horse. He remembered being thrown into a canyon, landing across a splintered log and knew he was lucky a lot more hadn't been damaged. Until it healed, however, the hole in his leg was going to be a miserable inconvenience he hadn't foreseen. It would end his tracking.

Nearly his whole herd had disappeared last week and he'd put every available man out to find them. He could only hope none of the crew had met a fate similar to his. He would have to see about mail service and send a message north to Bill, his foreman, and hope he was at the ranch to receive it. *In the meantime, God, I'm presuming there was a good reason for this detour so I'll keep my crankiness to myself and be grateful that good woman found me. I wish heartily you could shed some light on why my herds are the ones being raided. If something isn't done soon, I'm going to be ruined.*

A certain amount of rustling had to be tolerated. Other ranches on the northern boundary of the Shoshone reservation had not escaped either, but his losses were by far the greatest. No, there was more to the rustling than the surface indicated.

And he didn't believe for one minute that his cattle were the best around as Jed Skyler had said. As the Indian agent, Jed and his wife lived on the reservation far to the south of Dan's ranch and not too distant from Parke's Crossing. Dan had stopped there a couple of days ago before riding into the Owl Mountains. It was in the foothills of those mountains where he had been thrown from his horse.

A dog barked, shattering the quiet night and Dan's thoughts. Dan put his ear to the earth floor beside his bed and heard the soft thud of approaching footsteps. Dan quickly feigned sleep as the door creaked open and someone stepped inside.

The stove blocked Carrie's line of sight as she approached her patient. She circled around and turned up the lamp. Apprehension at what she might find caused her hand to tremble slightly. She had changed the bandage on Dan's wound twice already, and still it continued to seep blood. He had remained unconscious each time and that concerned her. He must drink and eat soon or the fever would consume him.

Kneeling beside him, Carrie saw the slow rise of Dan's eyelids as he stirred and blinked in the brighter light. *Thank you, Lord,* she breathed silently.

Carrie asked softly, "Want some water?"

Dan nodded.

She disappeared and returned shortly with a full bucket. A tin cup clicked softly against the side of it as she walked. She set it down beside him. He refused her offer of help, so Carrie only watched as he filled the cup. Too weak to raise his head sufficiently, Dan spilled most of the water down his shirt front as he drank.

Wordlessly, she reached for a towel and mopped up the spill.

Sheepish at his failure, he avoided her eyes. "You been in here earlier tonight?" he asked in a hoarse voice as he hung the cup on the bucket.

"Yes," came Carrie's brief reply. There was an underlying ferocity about this unknown man that made her guarded.

He cleared his throat. "Name's King."

"I know." She smoothed his blankets. "Are you warm enough?"

"Fine."

She followed his eyes as he looked about at the dismal, crudely-built cabin with strips of bark curling off the log walls.

"Where am I?" he asked at last.

"Parke's Crossing."

"No, this room."

"Benson Hotel's wash house. I found you and brought you in."

"Who are you?"

He obviously had no memory of their earlier conversation. "Carrie Benson," she said gently.

They were interrupted by the rattle of the door latch. Carrying a tray, Elsa entered the room. Her short neck was set deep in her shoulders and bowed in a manner

14

reminiscent of a charging bull. She stood just inside the door looking at Dan, making no effort to hide her hostility. Then her eyes shifted to Carrie.

"He worse?" she asked as she crossed to Dan's bedside.

"He's fine." Carrie's eyes drifted to the tray in Elsa's hands. "What have you fixed? It smells awfully tempting."

"Just soup still warm from supper. I thought it would give him strength and help get him out of here faster," Elsa answered, sniffing her displeasure at Dan's presence and ignoring him.

"Your days is long enough without nursing a penniless drifter half the night," she said. Her words sounded solicitous of Carrie, but the tone of voice held an edge of authority.

Elsa finally acknowledged Dan. "You get soup tonight, but let's get something straight, Dan King. Carrie's not standing over a hot stove all day cooking food to stoke into you."

Dan stared at the ceiling. "I don't recall mentioning the subject," he said, weariness engraving each word. "And I'm not penniless. I have a cattle ranch up north near Montana Territory."

"So you say," retorted Elsa.

Carrie sighed. "Please, Elsa, let him eat his soup so we can all get some sleep. We can settle this in the morning."

Dan shifted about so he could look intently at Carrie. She wished he wouldn't. She knew she looked far from her best. Not that she was beautiful, but she did have good skin and a small, well-shaped nose. Her fingers fluttered to the thick, sand-colored hair swept back in two neat wings to a fancy knot on the nape of her neck, and she permitted a slight smile to lift the corners of her mouth.

Still glaring at Dan, Elsa refused to be placated. "No, we'll settle it now." Handing the tray to Carrie, Elsa continued, "Carrie'd feed and quarter every drifter between here and the North Platte for free. Thinks she's the good samaritan for all this part of Wyoming Territory. *I* want to know, can you pay?"

Dan's eyes grew cautious. "Some," he said.

"All right. Carrie'll take care of you 'til your money runs out. You'd better be well enough to travel by then," she warned, shaking her finger at him for emphasis. Satisfied that she had made her point, Elsa whirled and stalked across the room. After one final hard look, she slammed out the door.

"Don't mind Elsa," Carrie said as she knelt to set the tray on the floor. "She's the closest thing to a mother I've had since my own family was killed in a stagecoach accident eight years ago. I was sixteen at the time.

"She takes the responsibility very seriously. Gets a little blunt when she thinks I'm being put upon, but she means well. Doesn't want anyone to know she's soft as fresh butter under all that crust."

As Carrie rolled up an extra pillow and, with a practiced hand tucked it under Dan's head, she felt his eyes on her again. She tried to shrug off the weariness which slumped her shoulders, but too many hours since morning and too much work made the effort short-lived.

Carrie rested back on her heels and folded her hands in her lap. "When you've had your fill of looking," she said calmly, "I'll set the tray so you can eat."

A dark blush, visible even in the poor light, spread over his face. "Sorry. Didn't mean to be rude. Just been a long while since I've seen a beautiful lady. My manners slipped.

The scent of lilacs has always been my favorite. Reminds me of my mother." A slight southern accent shaped his words.

Carrie uncovered the tray and any scent of lilacs was quickly overwhelmed by the aroma of onions and fresh bread as she set the food beside him.

Dan closed his eyes briefly, then attacked the thick potato soup and warm bread.

Carrie fussed around tidying an already orderly room until he finished.

"More?" she asked.

Dan didn't pretend. "Haven't eaten for a couple of days."

Wordlessly she gathered the tray, left, and returned with a steaming refill. Still ravenous, Dan cleaned up the second portion, and looked up at Carrie who stood watching him.

His brief scowl told her he had caught her look of concern before she could clear it from her face. "Your injury isn't that serious," she said, attempting to reassure him. "You'll be uncomfortable and not able to ride for awhile is all."

"You always read minds?" he asked.

Carrie laughed softly. "Just some people's."

Quickly she sought a different subject of conversation. "Not much supper I'm afraid. Hotel's full and they cleaned up everything. We'll do better by you tomorrow."

"You couldn't. Best meal I've had in ages."

She chuckled softly. "Hunger makes any woman a good cook."

She gathered the tray, preparing to leave, but Dan seemed determined to keep her there. Carrie knew that life on the isolated ranches got very lonely for the men without wives. She had been told that sometimes the need for gentle company was as great as the need for food.

Dan raised up on his elbow and propped his head on his hand. "I see you keep a rifle handy in the corner, and Elsa seems nervous as a caged cat," he said. "Trouble brewing down this way, too, I take it?"

Carrie's eyes flashed to the gun blurred by the shadows. "Elsa says there is. I haven't seen anything but some smoke signals. Can't read their messages, though. Keeps me feeling uneasy."

"Never have known smoke-talk to bring good news. Do you know how to shoot that?" Dan motioned to the gun with his hand.

"Not as well as I'd like. Too busy to practice."

"Maybe things'll slow down. I'll be having some free time for the next few days." He glanced down at the leg lying immobile under its white bandage. "Glad to give you some lessons."

She smiled at him. "I'll think on your offer. Do you want your holster and shell belt?" She started toward where they lay on the table.

"Place looks safe enough," Dan said, permitting a slight grin. Then, changing the subject, he asked, "The man who helped carry me in last night . . . . What do you know about him? He a regular in town?"

"Phil Hardesty? A *real* fixture. Think he'd like the place named for him if the truth were known."

"You don't seem terribly fond of him."

Carrie blushed. She had tried to keep her dislike from showing.

"He never does anything until he calculates what's in it for him, and he takes advantage of those who need help. I can't prove anything; I just don't trust him. Just don't feel right when he's around."

Carrie didn't mention all the times Phil had hinted at marriage. When giving reasons for their union he'd always list their combined assets and the power it would give them. Never a word about love and children.

Dan didn't say anything, and seeing weariness growing in him Carrie gathered the tray, bid him good night, and took the lamp with her, leaving Dan in darkness.

Since Dan was obviously a stranger to the area, she couldn't help wondering as she returned the tray to the hotel kitchen what his interest in Hardesty was.

Chapter 2

The few dishes could wait until morning, Carrie decided as she placed them in the dishpan, picked up a small oil lamp and slowly mounted the stairs. Treading softly so as not to disturb her sleeping guests, she arrived at the top step where the yellow circle of light flickered over a tall woman clutching desperately at the wall. The woman swayed unsteadily along the dark corridor, rich auburn hair straggled over her face. Her stylish clothes hung in disarray.

"Alice Skyler, what are you doing here—and in that condition?" Carrie gasped and made a quick grab to keep Alice on her feet.

"Wanna sleep," Alice mumbled and dropped her head on Carrie's shoulder.

In her exhausted state, Carrie swayed under the weight and both women nearly fell. "I haven't an empty bed tonight, Alice." Carrie felt tears sting the back of her eyelids as she thought about sharing her single bed, knowing she would sleep little in such crowded circumstances.

"You'll have to stay in my room. I'll put some quilts on the floor." Carrie wrapped a stabilizing arm around Alice's waist and began guiding her down the hall. Alice lurched, slamming both of them abruptly into the wall. A groan and profanity from the other side of the wall let Carrie know the occupant was not pleased with the intrusion into his sleep. The lamp nearly slipped from her hand. Frightened by the consequences of such an accident, she set the lamp on the floor and concentrated on maneuvering Alice through the dim corridor and into her back corner room.

"Hold on to the bedpost, Alice, while I spread the quilts."

She curled Alice's fingers around the support and hurried to the linen closet. When Carrie returned with the lamp and quilts, she found Alice collapsed across the bed. No amount of effort would budge the snoring woman.

"Oh, how I'd like to take a horse whip to the person who gets that liquor for you!" Carrie muttered as she looked down into the once-beautiful face, now puffy and waxen. Even in sleep, the mouth remained set in a grim defiant line.

With a sigh, Carrie slipped into her nightgown and lay down on the quilt-covered floor. Exhaustion blanked her mind until she woke with the morning, stiff and sore.

Resting in the half-light of the pre-dawn, Carrie slowly reviewed yesterday's events. Dan King's wound was not from a gun shot. Yet, even wounded he sat his horse with too much expertise for something minor to have thrown him. He was obviously an accomplished horseman. He said he had some money, but she noticed his face stiffen slightly at the mention of it. His boots, guns, tack, and horse were the best, however that meant little. Most cowboys with any pride saved for and spent their last dime on these items. She wanted to convince herself he was just a drifter whose horse had stepped in a badger hole and unseated him, but still . . . .

Awkwardly crawling to her feet, she pushed tangled hair away from her face. She'd been too tired last night to brush and tie back the long thick strands as she usually did. Glancing at the bed, she saw that Alice still slept soundly. Her pale cheeks accentuated eyes sunk deep in their sockets and smudged underneath with dark circles.

Carrie shook her head in sorrow at her friend's plight and began her morning toilette and quiet time. Her day didn't seem to start right without a few minutes for Bible reading and prayers. If she waited until later in the day, her mind became too occupied to concentrate fully.

Elsa already had the bread mixed and rising when Carrie presented herself in the immaculate, well-equipped kitchen.

Flustered and embarrassed at the lateness of her arrival, Carrie only nodded a morning greeting and wordlessly pulled a large black iron skillet onto the stove. Adding hot bacon grease, she broke the shells and dropped freshly-laid eggs in to fry.

Footsteps of hungry men began echoing down the stairs and through the lobby. Dining room chairs scraped and squeaked as weight settled upon them. At this signal, Carrie picked up the big black pot of boiling coffee and went out to fill cups. There was a minimum of talk as cowboys, freighters and a couple of soldiers sat at the long oilcloth-covered dining table awaiting their food.

Years ago Carrie had learned to remain silent until after

the second cup of coffee and a portion of the bacon, eggs, fried potatoes, and biscuits had been consumed. Gradually, sleep-rasped voices cleared and a low steady rumble droned through the room.

"Carrie, hear tell some drifter wandered in and is sleeping in the wash house. That true?" one of the soldiers asked.

She fixed him with an unflinching gaze. "With a hotel full of beds, why would I put someone in the wash house?"

Even as she answered, Carrie wondered why she evaded his question. It was certainly no secret that she had such a man on the premises. The whole town had witnessed his arrival.

"That's what I said when they told me. So you don't have a wounded man there?" the soldier pursued. "We bin lookin' for a drifter supplyin' the Indians with whiskey."

All attention focused on her while her eyes slowly circled the table. *What on earth am I going to say?* Her unwillingness to reveal Dan's whereabouts puzzled her deeply, particularly if he *was* smuggling the forbidden liquor.

From the kitchen doorway Elsa's sharp voice cracked unexpectedly across the room. "You want to check the wash house?" The words were issued as a challenge.

"N .. n .. no, I guess not," the young man stammered. "If you say he's not there, that's good enough for me."

Elsa shrugged and stepped back into the kitchen.

Forgive me, Lord, for the evasion, Carrie prayed, not understanding why she and Elsa had perpetrated it, but extremely grateful to Elsa for rescuing her.

When the guests were fed and gone, Carrie brought out her special silver tray from the pantry. Why did Dan King's presence matter and why should it be kept from the soldier? She pondered this again while she took extra pains in preparing his breakfast.

Carrie felt Elsa's eyes boring into her back. "I know you took Christ into your life years ago and vowed to follow His ways and it isn't my place to tell you what to do," Elsa said, prefacing her coming lecture, "but we've got mounds of dishes and laundry. This hardly seems the day to dawdle over a waste of skin like Dan King. Like as not, he's already up and gone without leaving any pay for yesterday."

Banging the dishpan onto the stove, Elsa filled it with water from the barrel in the corner, then gave her hands a thorough wiping on a fresh, red-striped apron.

"Like as not," Carrie agreed amiably as she folded one of her best linen napkins beside the fine china and covered the silver tray with another. "But if you feel like that about him, why didn't you tell the trooper where Dan was sleeping?"

Elsa sniffed and snatched up a basket. Mumbling something about getting potatoes from the root cellar, she disappeared through the door.

Carrie smiled. Elsa couldn't bear to be caught in a kindly act. She worked hard at the crusty reputation she enjoyed.

As Carrie finished making up his breakfast tray, she allowed her thoughts to slip back to Dan. Anyone could say they owned a ranch, but somehow coming from him it sounded like the truth. At any rate, she didn't think he was a drifter. There was something different about him. Something that made her feel desirable, honored, and respected. Not many men made Carrie feel anything and certainly not when she knew as little about them as she did this man. She picked up the tray and carried it to the wash house, her heart pulsing in her throat.

At her entrance, Dan stirred. "Good morning," he said, pushing himself into a sitting position. Long, well-shaped fingers raked sleep-tossed hair from his eyes and a shy grin greeted her.

"How's the leg?" she asked.

He flexed it carefully. "That fiery liniment and tight bandage have done the job," he answered.

She placed the tray next to him. "Still hurt?"

"Just an ache now. Nothing I can't handle."

While Dan ate, Carrie built a fire in the black stove, set the boiler on, and filled it from the large barrel of rain water standing in a corner. There was no conversation between them, but Carrie felt a contentment in their silence.

As Dan finished eating, she watched him wipe his mouth, then finger the finely loomed napkin a moment as a faraway look stole briefly into his eyes. Slowly he folded one napkin and carefully covered the tray with the other, leaving it as she had served it except for the empty dishes.

"Real good," he said in a husky whisper. "Real good." Then, holding out a hand, he asked, "Mind giving me some help?" His voice, with an undertone of steel in it, once more became brisk and impersonal.

Stunned by his request, it took a moment before Carrie could answer. "What do you think you're going to do?" she asked sharply.

"I'm going to get on my feet and walk out of here," he said in a quiet, steady way.

His jaw was set and Carrie now knew the square shape *was* an indication of stubbornness. Well, her own jaw line was far from weak!

"I've invested considerable time and effort on your behalf," she said with a firmness equaling his. "Stand on that leg and start it bleeding again, and I'll flatten you and tie you down."

To back up her words, she glanced toward the rifle still propped in the corner.

His eyes followed hers. "Since you plan to keep me an immobile prisoner, what provisions are you going to make for the relief of certain other biological needs besides hunger?" His eyes, twinkling mischievously, caught hers and his lips turned upward into the beginnings of a smile.

Struck by the implication of his remarks and her own thoughtlessness, she lowered her head in an attempt to hide the blush already beginning to heat her face. "I believe there's an old crutch around somewhere. Can you wait 'til I find it?"

"I'll try." Feigned innocence spread over his face before he gave her a slow, wicked wink.

Thoroughly flustered, Carrie hurried from the room, grateful to escape his amused glances.

When she returned with a well-used crutch left by a long-forgotten hotel guest, Dan was sitting on the edge of the mattress trying to stand.

"Here," she said, offering her hand. He took it and pulled hard against her. "Easy now," she cautioned.

Slowly Dan raised himself to his full height and caught his breath.

"Hurt?" she asked.

He merely nodded and placed the too-short crutch under his arm. He leaned on the support, grasped the handhold and, holding his injured leg off the floor, tried a step. Then, with Carrie shadowing his every move, he hobbled reasonably well about the room. The heat from the stove was making the room stifling, and Carrie wished she could open the window. But she didn't dare stop now lest she not be there if he grew weak and started to topple.

26

"If you'll hand me my hat, I'll be on my way," he said.

She retrieved the dusty Stetson from the corner where it had f llen when Phil had laid Dan on the mattress. Finding a cloth, she wiped it off before handing it to him. "You sure you're all right? Doesn't your leg ache?"

"It throbs, but no more than I can stand." He clamped the hat over chestnut-colored hair darker than his mustache. He hobbled slowly toward the door, then outside into the morning sunshine.

Carrie watched him disappear down the well-used path leading around the corner of the hotel before she turned back to recover the breakfast tray and leave. Starting up the steps to the kitchen, she remembered the soldier's inquiry and waited for Dan to return.

As he placed his crutch on the bottom step in preparation for climbing the stairs, she said, "There's a soldier inside asking about you. Any reason he should be curious?"

Dan's eyes narrowed in thought as he glanced at her. "Can't think of any. Ask for me by name, did he?"

"No, only asked about the drifter I'm supposed to have sleeping in my wash house."

"Give any clue to why he was interested in me?"

"He's looking for the person selling whiskey to the Indians."

"Soldier still around?"

"No. He and the other Army men rode south as soon as they finished eating."

"No need to defend my innocence right now, then." He appeared to change his mind about entering the hotel, turned away from Carrie and continued his lurching gait toward the trading post instead.

Carrie watched his laborious progress across the street

27

as he halted often to rest. Fortunately, there was little morning traffic beyond an occasional freight wagon and the people from her hotel riding out of town.

Each time he rested Carrie knew he studied the little town. The sprawling log trading post was an imposing building and, next to her hotel, the largest building around. Small cabins huddled near them like chicks around a mother hen. Some of the settlement cabins were new, built by isolated ranchers who wanted protection for their families against the Shoshone. Other cabins, perhaps a dozen in all, nestled comfortably under the few giant cottonwoods that dotted the town.

It is a nice town, Carrie thought. It suited her and she liked it . . . liked it fine except for the tensions which kept everyone's nerves on edge lately. The unnatural number of strangers and soldiers coming and going kept everyone's mind on the Indian unrest.

As Dan approached the Post, Phil came outside and sank into a barrel chair on the veranda. He watched as Dan swung around the hitching rail and arrived at the bottom of the three veranda steps. Heaving his bulk from the chair, Phil came to the edge of the top step. Holding out a hand he asked pleasantly enough, "Help you?"

The wind carried the conversation to Carrie as she walked around the hotel to have an unobstructed view of the trading post. She began sweeping the morning's accumulation of dust from the front steps and porch.

Carrie continued to watch Dan out of the corner of her eye as he grasped the rail, steadied himself, and said, "I'll make it fine." Slowly, painfully it appeared, he climbed the steps. Without stopping to rest after the top step, Dan started across the veranda on his way inside.

Phil, who had watched every movement, now suggested, "Why don't you sit down?" The older man shoved a chair forward. "I'll get whatever it is you want."

Dan halted, propped his crutch against the wall, and sank into the offered chair. He rubbed the injured leg and wiped his sleeve across his forehead.

"You work here?" Dan asked.

"I own it. Name's Phil Hardesty."

Silence hung in the morning air, punctuated only by hammer blows from the forge in the livery down the street.

"Come for anything special?" Phil asked at last.

Dan nodded. "Wondered if you carried crutches. This one's borrowed, and it's built for a shorter fellow. From the feel, I'm going to be needing help for longer than I can manage on it."

"Always keep a couple on hand. Just for emergencies." Hardesty disappeared inside the dark interior of the store.

Sweat from Dan's exertion made his shirt front dark with irregular splotches. He closed his eyes and Carrie watched his body sag.

Presently, Phil came out of the store with a tall crutch and leaned it against the wall next to the one Dan had been using. He swung back into the chair he'd recently vacated and offered Dan a cigar. Dan declined, but Phil lighted up. Over the flare of the match he watched Dan, sizing up his distress and vulnerability. Neither man spoke while the air filled with acrid blue smoke.

At last Phil spoke. "I put the charge for the crutch on an account. You can turn it back for credit when you leave."

Dan nodded his approval.

"You from around here?" Phil asked. "I don't recall seein' you before."

Again Dan slowly shook his head without speaking.

"Indians gun you down...or did you run into more trouble than you could handle?"

Dan's body tensed at the inference. "What trouble might that be?" he asked, his tone calm.

"Oh, I hear tell there's been a whole lot of rustlin' up north. Most say it's Indians. I say not. More likely some eager cowboys anxious to start a herd the cheap way."

Was it Carrie's imagination or did Phil's explanation sound too smooth? Almost as if it had been rehearsed for Dan's benefit?

Phil changed the subject. "How's Carrie treating you?" he asked idly.

"Fine," Dan returned, his voice unreadable.

"That old dragon, Elsa, try to boot you out on your ear?" Phil chuckled. "Hates to have an eligible man within a hundred miles of Carrie. Gets right menacing when she senses danger."

"Why should *she* care?" Dan asked.

Phil grimaced. "Got a good thing goin' at the hotel. Can't afford to buy it, but she runs the place and Carrie. If Carrie was to get married and sell out, Elsa's days would be numbered. Nobody else would put up with her foul disposition."

Carrie seethed at Phil's remarks and only by the greatest effort kept from dashing across the street to throw his words in his face.

As Phil concluded his opinions, raised voices from the store punctuated the morning quiet. Phil listened a minute, then, reacting to the trouble, rose and stormed across the veranda to stand in the doorway looking inside.

"What's the ruckus?" he demanded.

A disheveled woman scooped tresses of thick red hair

out of her eyes as she swept past Phil and out onto the veranda.

"Alice!" Carrie gasped and quickly leaned the broom against the hotel wall.

Turning back to Phil, Alice begged, "Please make him give me a drink." Her speech was slurred and she swayed slightly. "I'll give you . . . him . . . anything you want."

Carrie started across the street. "Oh, Alice," she whispered, "Why? Why?"

Hardesty's eyes took on a hard glitter and he gave a brittle laugh. "Jed know where you are and what you're doing?" he asked. "How many times I told you to stay away from my place? You're gettin' to be a real pest and bad for business."

Confusion twisted her face. "But you said . . . " she began thickly.

An angry voice from inside the room interrupted, "You been told over and over you can't have liquor, Alice Skyler. I don't know where you keep gettin' it, but you ain't gettin' none from me!" A rumpled little man glared out the doorway at the distraught woman. "I swear to it, Mr. Hardesty."

"It's all right, Willie. I don't blame you." Phil waved aside the bartender's anxiety and nodded for him to go back inside.

When Carrie arrived at the foot of the trading post steps, Dan straightened in his chair. His injured leg remained stiff before him. Anger and alcohol contorting her features, Alice doubled her fists and slammed them against Phil's chest as hard as she could. He looked down and laughed in her face. She let loose a cry of fury and savagely kicked out at him. Phil easily side-stepped her foot and it landed squarely on Dan's outstretched, wounded leg.

For a second, Dan looked as though he would faint from the purest of agony. He struggled to stand and get away from the drink-crazed woman. He thrust himself out of the chair with his arms, tipping it over as he wheeled on his one good leg. He leaped for the wall and his crutch. Alice, thrown off-balance, lurched and tripped over the chair Dan had just vacated. She sprawled, head first off the veranda, landing in the dusty street at Carrie's feet.

Carrie saw Dan collapse against the wall, swaying as if he would sink to the veranda floor at any second. Sweat streamed down his face as he fought to remain upright. He shook his head repeatedly as though trying to clear it.

Torn between whom to help first, Carrie was distracted further by the awareness that Phil Hardesty was raking her with his eyes. She was positive he was giving Alice the liquor, but she was unable to prove it. Carrie glared at him and her dislike burned in her eyes.

Dan finally steadied himself, but his head hung down so she couldn't see his face. Seeing him upright, Carrie knelt beside the prostrate woman.

"Alice," she said, shaking her. The only answer was a low moan. "Alice, you have to get up and I can't lift you."

Carrie looked up to see Phil standing in the doorway watching. Though it curdled her insides, she said, "Phil, please help me get her over to the hotel."

His eyes narrowed at her request. "She's down there because of her own actions."

"I know, but we can't leave her. Please, Phil," Carrie begged.

His only reply was to fold his arms over his chest and survey the scene with apparent detachment.

Instinctively, she switched her gaze to Dan. He lifted his face, pale as rising dough, then slumped back against the wall.

Dear God, she prayed. *What am I to do? There are two people who need me.* She managed to roll Alice over and lift her to a sitting position. Maybe she could at least drag Alice out of the street. By getting behind Alice and lifting her slightly, Carrie managed to drag the unconscious woman back to the steps of the veranda. She paused to catch her breath and mop away the perspiration beading on her forehead.

"Hardesty," a dull voice behind Carrie said. "Help her or I'll send this crutch into your mid-section."

Carrie glanced quickly over her shoulder to see Dan, standing straight, with the second crutch raised and aimed.

Phil sent Dan an amused look, shrugged, and descended the steps. Roughly, he gathered Alice into his arms.

"Take her to Carrie's hotel," Dan ordered in his quiet, steel-like voice. He pushed away from the wall and prepared to follow Phil down the steps.

Carrie ran ahead to find a bed for Alice, and when they arrived she stood at the top of the stairs. "Bring her up here," she said.

Phil paused for breath and threw Alice over his shoulder. Her head bounced against his belt and she groaned.

"Take it easy, Hardesty!" Dan warned.

Carrie realized that, even in his weakened condition, Dan wasn't a man to be taken lightly. And though Phil made light of Dan's threat, he had responded to her request without further discussion. He must have sensed it, too.

The strange procession haltingly made its way up the stairs and into a room at the top. Phil flopped the drunken woman onto an unmade bed. After dusting himself off, he brought out a fresh handkerchief and mopped the perspiration from his forehead and from around his neck.

Both Phil and Carrie stood watching as Alice curled into a fetal position and rocked back and forth, moaning softly.

"Thanks, Phil," Carrie tried to make her voice warm.

"Yeah," he said ungraciously. "When you gonna get her out of town? I don't need no more scenes like this."

The muscles in Carrie's jaw clenched. "Don't worry yourself, Phil. Alice will be gone by tonight."

"She better be," was his parting remark as he pounded down the stairs and slammed the door, sending angry echoes throughout the hotel.

Chapter 3

Carrying a supper tray, Carrie swung open the door to Alice's room and felt the rush of hot, stale air. The room faced the west and, in her earlier haste, she had forgotten to pull the blind against the afternoon sun. Alice was still sprawled over the bed, sleeping soundly.

Carrie set the tray on the dresser. Shaking Alice, she said, "Come on, Alice. Wake up and eat something. I'm sure it's been days since you had anything solid."

Alice groaned and moved closer to the wall.

"That won't do, Alice. Come on, please," Carrie begged, but Alice curled into a tight ball and refused to budge.

"Looks like you've got a problem," Dan said quietly from the open doorway.

Startled, Carrie whirled about. "How did you get up here?" she asked.

"I took off my shirt, spread my wings and flew," he said

with a grin, still panting from the labor of his climb.

She returned his smile. "I deserved that."

"I saw you come up and thought you might need some help. May I come in?"

At first Carrie hesitated, then said, "Why not? It's not the first time she's slept off a drunk without privacy."

Dan pushed away from the door frame and hobbled over to stare down at the figure on the brass bed. "The first time I saw her she was traveling up north with Jed. Thought then she was a real beauty," he said solemnly. "Too bad she got into liquor." A sadness spread over his face.

"Where do you know Jed and Alice from?" Carrie asked in surprise.

"From the agency. Just about everyone in these parts knows them."

Her curiosity satisfied, Carrie said sadly, "Alice didn't drink when she first came here. She and Jed stayed in the hotel while they remodeled the house on the reservation. We got to be good friends. I've really missed her since they moved back about nine months ago."

Carrie turned to the oak washstand where she poured cold water from a flowered porcelain pitcher into the matching basin.

"Five of us women here in Parke's Crossing meet once a week to study the Bible, share our problems, and pray about them." Dampening a washcloth, Carrie sat on the edge of the bed to wash Alice's hands.

"Alice seemed seriously interested in the Bible and attended our studies regularly until about the time they moved. Then she started making excuses and her times at our meetings grew farther and farther apart. One night when Jed was away on business, I found her curled up, drunk and asleep, outside my bedroom door. The time between bouts has grown less and the quantity of her indulgence has increased ever since. I wish I knew who's getting the whiskey for her or why she needs it."

"Why does she come to town to get drunk?"

"Can't get liquor on the reservation, you know."

"I do, indeed. Keep forgetting she lives there."

"Jed doesn't seem aware of her problem or doesn't care. He's gone a great deal of the time and this leaves Alice free to come to town whenever she feels the urge. I sober her up and try to sneak her back before Jed returns and misses her, praying each time will be the last."

Carrie stood with a sigh and straightened her plain blue dress. "I need to get some food into her and see if Elsa will help me take her home."

Dan cast a disparaging look at his leg and crutch. "I realize I'm not all I could be, but with the Indians acting up, a rifle might be of some comfort on the trip to the reservation. Do you have a buggy?"

"Yes, but I'd prefer waiting until dusk, if you don't mind. Even though the whole town knows of Alice's problem, I still try to keep the matter as private as possible."

"Fine. I've no place to go. Couldn't go if I had," Dan said humorously.

Once again Carrie looked at the huddled figure on the coverlet. "If we can get her out of bed, it would be easier to wash and feed her."

Somehow they placed the limp, drowsy Alice in the small wicker rocking chair next to the bed. Breathless and pale from the exertion, Dan leaned against the bedstead, favoring his leg.

Carrie noticed and said, "I can take care of Alice. You need to give that leg a rest. Keep overdoing and you'll be no help later on."

Dan nodded, eased onto the rumpled bed, and

propped up his injured leg.

Throwing a towel over her shoulder, Carrie brought the basin to the bedside table. She washed Alice's face, brushed her hair, and pinned it up.

"Now, Alice, my dear, you are going to have to wake up and eat." She slapped Alice's cheeks smartly, and Alice began to fight her.

"That's a girl. Open your eyes and see who this is," Carrie said, encouraging her.

At last Alice peered reluctantly through slitted lids. "Carrie, is that you?" she asked in a weak voice.

"It's me, right enough. I've brought you some broth and fresh bread." Carrie uncovered the tray and held out a slice of buttered bread.

Alice turned her head away. "I can't," she said in a voice near tears.

"Then let me spoon some broth into you. You must eat."

"I know, I know." Alice took a sip of the offered broth and dutifully swallowed it.

By distracting Alice with the tale of how Dan King had ridden into Parke's Crossing, Carrie was able to feed her the soup without further problems.

"Now that you've eaten, you'll be better able to stand the trip to the reservation," Carrie said as she straightened the room.

"Do I have to go back?" Alice finally whimpered. "I don't want to go. I want to stay here with you."

"I don't think Jed would like that arrangement."

"I don't think he'd even notice," Alice said, a bitter tinge coloring her words.

Carrie raised her eyes and met Dan's. Though Carrie talked further about Jed's concern over Alice's disappearance, Alice said nothing more as she ate the rest of the broth.

By using her most persuasive manner, Carrie induced Alice to eat the bread. When she had finished, Dan stood up to leave with Carrie. Alice barely managed the two steps to the bed, then crumpled in a heap once more.

"If she lies down until we're ready to leave, I think she'll have enough strength for the trip," Carrie said as she collected the dishes.

Dan hobbled after her and shut the door. "Don't you ever get tired of nursing people?" he asked gently.

She smiled up at him. "No. It's one of the good things in my life, to be able to help," she said, starting down the stairs in front of him. About halfway down she realized she was walking alone and turned to see him standing at the head of the stairs. "Aren't you coming?"

"Not until you're clear. If I fall, I don't want you in the way."

"What a pleasant thought!" Nevertheless, she hurried downstairs and waited a safe distance from the bottom step until he navigated the stairs.

"I'll see to the buggy," Dan volunteered. "Be at the kitchen door just before dark." He nodded to her and limped out the front door.

"And I'll see if Elsa will come," Carrie called after him.

Even in the middle of summer, it grew chilly when the sun set behind the western mountains. Though it was too small, Carrie brought one of her capes for Alice as they prepared to leave. Draping it over Alice's shoulders, Carrie said, "It isn't grand, but it will keep you comfortable," and tied the ribbon into a bow at Alice's throat.

Alice stood quietly letting Carrie help her. "The cape's worth more than I am," she muttered.

"Won't you tell me why you continue to drink? After every spell, you always feel the same about yourself." Carrie produced a short-billed black bonnet and set it on Alice's auburn curls.

Alice took the ties from Carrie and, with shaking hands, attempted a bow.

"I *don't* feel the same about myself. I feel worse." She ignored Carrie's question.

"Then why do it?" Carrie persisted as she lifted the ribbons from fumbling fingers and deftly made an attractive bow in front of Alice's right ear.

Giving a great sigh, Alice answered, "Because I don't know what else to do."

Her voice was so pathetic Carrie wanted to cry. "Alice, you know God wants to help you. If you feel you can't tell anyone else, won't you turn to Him?"

"Don't you think I've tried to pray? But my prayers leave my heart like lead and fall in dull thuds at my feet. God wouldn't want me either," Alice whispered.

There was a long pause before she continued. "You can't imagine how awful it is. When I can't stand the pain anymore, I have a drink. I promise myself it will only be one, but I feel a bit better after one, so I think another one will help even more. It does take away the pain, but then when I wake up like this, I feel so guilty I want to die."

"It doesn't remove the guilt, Alice. Only Christ can do that. Alcohol only blurs it. The pain and the guilt will always be there until you do something about the cause. Can't you tell someone what's troubling you?"

"If I could, don't you think I would?" Abruptly turning her back on Carrie, Alice stooped to look in the mirror. Running her fingers lightly over the puffs under her eyes and along the deep creases on either side of her mouth, she first grimaced at the sight, then averted her eyes.

40

Carrie felt thoroughly rebuffed and helpless. What secret did Alice hold in her heart that was so terrible she couldn't turn to the Lord and let Him take care of it?

Dan's arrival at the back door of the hotel with Carrie's buggy brought welcome relief to the tense scene. Carrie threw a shawl over her shoulders, knocked on Elsa's door as she and Alice passed, and the three women walked quickly through the hotel.

In the waning light, the horses swung their heads around, curious at the approach of their passengers. Alice claimed Carrie's steadying hand and eased into the front seat. Dan got out of Carrie's buggy and double-checked Alice's rig tied to the back.

Elsa was last, grumbling as she went. "Such goings on!" she said, speaking as though Alice couldn't hear. "If that woman has to drink, wisht she'd do it in the privacy of her home and spare us such trouble." With a loud grunt, she hoisted her bulk into the back seat.

Wishing she could tie a gag in Elsa's mouth, Carrie spread a lap robe over Alice, then climbed into the back and sat as far from Elsa as the narrow seat allowed.

Patting the rifle beside him, Dan picked up the reins. "You in all right?" he asked Carrie.

She nodded, and he pulled the team around the hotel and started up the road toward the reservation. Holding the reins loosely in his big hands, he relaxed in the seat. As full night came, the gibbous moon bulged in the sky and lighted their way. A cool breeze from the mountains brought with it the scent of newly fallen rain in the high country.

For the first time in days, Carrie had nothing to do and she sat back to enjoy the tranquil ride. She liked having Dan King driving her buggy. Liked his strength. She had never been with anyone who could make a silence so meaningful. It was nice not to have to say everything outloud.

The rhythmic plop of the horses' hooves lulled Carrie into a light sleep and she jumped when a horse whinnied nearby. At the sound, the pace of the team quickened and moments later the buggy dipped over a rise and down into a shallow valley. The hour trip seemed to have taken no time at all. But Carrie's heart dropped at the sight that greeted them. Every window in the agency house glowed with light. Saddled horses stood everywhere around the modest, whitewashed clapboard house. *There goes any hope of Alice slipping in undetected,* she thought in dismay.

"Just stop at the hitching post. Don't bother to tie up and get out," Alice said, throwing back the robe as they drew close to the house.

Dan stopped as she instructed, but haltingly made his way around the buggy to assist her. Alice's feet touched the ground just as the wide front door flew open and Jed Skyler stepped out into the rectangle of lamplight shining through the opening.

His shadow stretched huge and almost formless across the porch and out onto the dust of the yard. Matted straw-colored hair contrasted with the dark tan of his skin. Hard angular shoulders pressed against a dirt-streaked white shirt. Carrie couldn't read his narrow face hidden in the shadows, but her heart beat ragged and irregular at the thought of what he might do to Alice.

"Speak up! Who ya be?" Jed shouted.

"King. Dan King. Carrie Benson and I have brought Alice home from a little trip to town."

Dan with a firm hand on Alice's arm limped toward Jed. "Looks like you're having a party. Sorry to interrupt, but we won't stay," Dan said and began slowly guiding Alice toward the porch steps.

"You're welcome to come on in and join us. Just a few of the boys from the ranches around close. Over for an evening of cards."

Jed glared at Alice. "Needed some entertainment since my wife wasn't home," he added with a sneer in his voice.

As he moved to the edge of the steps, Alice reached the top. "Glad to see you're sober enough to make it up on your own."

Looking over Alice's head, he called to Carrie, "Thanks for sobering her up 'fore you brought her back. Been real embarrassin' to have her stagger in on my party."

Carrie felt like crying at the coldness of Alice's reception. No wonder she dreaded coming home!

Dan hesitated as if to say something, then just shrugged. " 'Night, Alice," he said, not moving.

"Yes, good night, Alice," Carrie called. Then she added, "Now don't forget your promise to come spend a few days with me real soon."

"I might be there sooner than you expect," Alice answered softly.

"Couldn't. I'll be expecting you every day."

Jed grabbed Alice's arm and shoved her into the house. She called back over her shoulder, "Wait, I have your . . . " but her words were cut short by the slamming of the door.

Carrie flinched at the sound, shivered, and climbed into the front seat of the buggy. Dan limped back to the buggy and reached across Carrie for the lap robe. He carefully tucked it around Elsa, who sat in silent disapproval in the back seat. Then he unhitched Alice's rig and tied her horse to the hitching rail before climbing back into Carrie's buggy.

"You don't suppose he'll hurt her, do you?" Carrie worried aloud.

Dan clucked the team into a brisk walk. "Not in front of all those men. By the time they're gone maybe he'll have calmed down."

Carrie nodded in hopeful agreement.

"Say, did you recognize any of the horses?" Dan asked.

Carrie thought carefully. "Now that you mention it, I don't recall having seen any of them around. Why?"

"Seemed a goodly number for an evening of cards. With all the rustling problems, I can't imagine the ranchers letting their men off the range. I wouldn't let mine go. And," Dan added in a low, tight voice, "if I don't find out who's behind this rustling and get it stopped soon, I won't be in the cattle business much longer."

"That what you were doing when you got hurt—tracking the rustlers?"

"Yep. Must have gotten too close, because I don't believe it was natural causes that spooked my horse."

"Think it's got anything to do with the Indian talk?"

"I don't know. I came down to see Skyler before I started tracking on my own. Thought he might have some answers, but he seemed as baffled as the rest of us."

"Why haven't I ever seen you around here before?"

"Do my business in Montana Territory. Don't recall ever being in your little town before, but I heard of it from Skyler."

They fell silent but sounds of the nocturnal creatures pricked at the night, giving it no rest. Carrie dozed until she felt Dan move in the seat. His soft moan jarred her fully awake. "Dan, what's the matter?"

"Leg's a little cramped. Nothing to fret about."

Carrie looked closely at him. Even accounting for the

effects of the moonlight, his lack of color frightened her. She looked down to see a dark stain on his pants leg.

"I should have had better sense than to let you come," she wailed. "If that leg doesn't heal properly, I'll never forgive myself."

"Leg'll be fine. We're almost to the hotel. Get it stretched out and put some of your infamous liniment on it. That and a night's sleep'll make it good as new."

"Not in that short a time, it won't. You're going to have to stay off it or it's not ever going to heal. Hear me?"

"Yes, ma'am."

She felt quite smug over his acceptance of her edict, but not for long.

"Don't suppose there's any work a fellow could do around the settlement?" he asked.

"A fellow isn't going to be in any condition to work for some time, so he doesn't need to concern himself," Carrie retorted.

"I haven't enough money with me that I can afford to pay for your services more than a couple of days. And Elsa says I can't live off your hospitality."

A loud "hummph" from the back seat let him know his jibe had found its mark.

"You leave Elsa out of this. You are *not* leaving until I say you're healed."

Dan slowed to a stop at the hotel. Carrie grabbed his crutch and jumped down. Hurrying around to his side, she helped him catch his balance and brace the crutch under his arm.

As they started for the wash house, he balked. "What about the team? They need to be put up."

"Don't you worry about that. I'll put them away when you're taken care of."

"Don't suppose it'll hurt me none to see to 'em," Elsa

said grudgingly as she crawled clumsily out of the buggy.

Carrie didn't argue but hurried into the wash house and lit the lamp sitting on the stove.

"You're right about Elsa," Dan said, noticing the fresh sheets on his bed. "She is a good woman." He eased down onto the bed and laid back on the stack of pillows.

After gathering the nursing supplies from a nearby shelf, Carrie unpinned Dan's pants leg to reveal the blood-spotted bandage. After removing the wrapping, she found it wasn't as bad as she had thought. She gave thanks that only one place had cracked open.

Carrie talked as she worked. "If you behave and don't do anything to upset Elsa, she'll recover her usual good humor soon."

Dan chuckled. "Phil Hardesty says she doesn't have any good humor."

"Where he's concerned, she doesn't. Neither do I. I know it's not Christian to feel toward another as I do toward him, but I just can't seem to overcome my intense dislike of that man."

"Being Christian doesn't mean we've arrived at perfection. Only means we're working toward it. I'm sure Phil has earned your disfavor. Mind telling me what he's done?"

Carrie eyed him in wonder as she poured liniment over the wound. Was Dan a Christian, too? Before she could ask, Dan's face knotted up in pain.

"Got to be the best medicine I ever had if inflicting pain is the measure," he gasped.

"It *is* good. Sorry it hurts so," Carrie said in sympathy. Gently, she wrapped new strips of sheeting around his leg and watched his face relax as the pain subsided.

"You ignoring my question about your dislike of

46

Hardesty?" he was finally able to ask.

"No. We sort of got sidetracked." She straightened her supplies as she sat on the foot of the bed. "Two reasons I don't like him. He tells everyone within earshot that he's going to marry me, so if anyone eligible does come along, they don't stay. He's also made it no secret that he wants my hotel. I've refused his offers to buy it so many times, he's quit trying. And that scares me. Phil isn't one to give up when he wants something. I keep wondering what he's planning."

"Sounds like a fine fellow," Dan muttered.

She set the kit back on the shelf and turned to him. "If you will *please* stay off it tomorrow, I can practically guarantee you a healed leg in a couple of weeks."

"Thanks. I'll make no promises, but I will have a good sleep tonight. That'll go a long way toward getting me off your hands."

Taking the lamp with her, Carrie wearily walked the short distance to the kitchen stairs. The hotel was dark and quiet. Elsa had apparently already gone to her room. As Carrie made her way upstairs, she worried over the reception Alice had received at home.

Chapter 4

Phil was in the hotel lobby when Carrie came downstairs the next morning.

"You're certainly up early," she greeted him, surprised by his presence and striving to make her voice pleasant. "Breakfast will be a while. Want a cup of coffee while you wait?"

Phil blocked Carrie's path to the kitchen. "Wanted to make sure you got back safely from your little trip last night." His eyes narrowed slightly, as though he could bore through her.

Carrie knew he watched her comings and goings, but she had no idea he kept such close track of her.

"With so many customers last night, how is it that you had time to keep track of my unimportant little excursions?" Her words were even and cool.

"I'm never too busy for that. Pretty, innocent thing like

you galavantin' around with the likes of Alice Skyler and that stranger could lead to trouble."

"I'm sure if there were any danger Elsa would smell it first thing and give me warning," Carrie said lightly as she tried to step around Phil. He moved with surprising quickness and Carrie found herself backed against the front desk, imprisoned between his burly arms.

"Phil, what are you doing?" she asked, trying to hide her rising alarm.

"Just making sure you understand whose girl you are."

"That's nonsense!" she exploded quietly, her voice low but intense. "You have no claim on me and never have had!" She grabbed one of his arms and attempted to push it out of the way.

He gave a wicked laugh. "Keep fightin', Carrie. I like my woman to have spirit. It'll make things a lot more interesting when we marry and I take you to the sweetest ranch in all of the Territory."

"I am *not* your woman, Phil Hardesty! And I'm not marrying you or living on any ranch with you! Now, you let me go or I'll scream. I don't think it would take the gentlemen upstairs long to get down here."

"There's not a gentleman in the lot and you know it. Besides, by the time any of 'em crawled out of bed to see about the commotion, you'd be standing here in the lobby alone. They'd wonder what got into you."

He chuckled, mean and low. Then grasping her face with one hand and encircling her waist with the other, he moved to close the gap between them.

"I'd hate to shoot you while you're standing so close to Carrie," Dan said in carefully measured words, "but if I have to, I will."

Carrie looked past Hardesty. Dan stood in the arch

between the dining room and lobby, a Colt .45 extended. There wasn't the slightest tremor in the hand holding the gun, and Carrie knew Dan would do exactly as he had threatened. Phil's grip slackened slightly, and she pulled back against the desk to allow as much room between them as possible.

The two men stared at each other. They reminded Carrie of two elk pawing the ground, each taking the measure of the other before crashing their horns together in a thundering fight.

"Hardesty! Move!" Dan's patience had apparently run out.

"Sure, sure. Don't get so riled. Me and Carrie's old friends." Phil's voice was smooth and slick as bear grease. As though trying to decide how serious Dan was about his threat, Phil still held Carrie but gave his full attention to the revolver.

Sensing his total involvement with Dan, Carrie gave Phil a hard shove. It surprised him enough that he loosened his grip and she darted past Dan into the dining room.

With Carrie out of the line of fire, Dan leaned heavily on his crutch and advanced one limping step toward Phil.

"Hardesty, if I *ever* see you take that kind of liberty with Miss Benson again, I'll see to it that it's a long while before you're able to try it a second time."

Phil paled and ran his hand through unruly hair. "She asked for it, King. What's a man to do when a comely woman throws herself at him? Be a shame to waste all those looks."

Phil openly let his eyes move down the length of Carrie. "She plays the saint with you, but she asked for it."

"Hardesty, you've got a filthy mouth! I saw the whole thing. All Carrie did was walk down the stairs and try to come through the lobby. Do you start every day this way, making a nuisance of yourself with Carrie?"

Phil didn't answer.

Dan turned to Carrie. "Does he?"

Carrie took several deep breaths, trying to control the racing beat of her heart. She had never had a man fight for her honor before and, while the thought of it was terribly frightening, it also gave her a feeling of security—a feeling she had nearly forgotten existed.

"Well?"

"Not often." Phil always found a way to make any eligible newcomer think that she belonged to him. Dan was the first to take issue with the scene she was sure had been staged for his benefit.

"Not often!" She saw the fire explode in Dan's eyes.

"It's all right, Dan. I can handle it," she said in an effort to calm him.

"Maybe you can. I can't! Hardesty, you stay away from her. Hear me!"

"Sure, Dan. Sure." Never taking his eyes from the revolver, Phil eased away from the desk. "If the lady don't want my attentions, I sure won't force 'em on her."

He wiped his palms down his pants legs. Looking past Dan to Carrie, he asked, "All right if I stay for breakfast?"

She nodded and broke for the kitchen. *No, he won't force himself on me until Dan King is gone. Then watch him get even.* Carrie's mouth parched at the thought of what lay in store for her. Suddenly, she wondered if the hotel and the security it offered were worth it. Maybe she should just sell out to Phil and run for it.

"Good morning, Elsa." Carrie hoped her voice sounded normal as she entered the kitchen.

"Mornin'. You're a mite late again. You need help wakin' up after all your night life?"

Carrie grinned in spite of herself. "No. Got in the middle

51

of a discussion between Phil and Dan in the lobby."

"What those two got to talk about? Lessen Dan's one of Phil's boys."

"I get the feeling Dan's his own man."

Elsa made no reply. Carrie busied herself slicing potatoes for frying while Elsa prepared the pancakes. As Carrie filled the hot pans with thick slices of ham, her thoughts returned to the earlier scene. *How had Phil known Dan would see him make his advances?* Carrie wondered as she cooked the tender smoked ham, its tempting aroma wafting through the hotel up to the rooms. There was one gratifying thing. There had been no witnesses to the scene so Phil wouldn't feel called on to vindicate himself. That just might save her.

The sound of scraping chairs alerted Carrie to the arrival of hungry guests. The aroma of the frying ham had done its job. Hungry men couldn't sleep with the smell of breakfast tickling their noses.

She carried the coffee pot into the dining room and began the morning ritual of filling the yawning cups set out around a silent table.

She nearly dropped the pot, however, when she saw Dan sitting across the table from Phil. The two men were deep in conversation, their voices so low Carrie couldn't catch any hint of the subject matter. Maybe Elsa had been right after all and Dan was partnering with Phil. Tears welled up inside and Carrie sniffed.

Then she thought again of the scene before breakfast. The anger in Dan had looked terribly real. If it wasn't, he was an extremely competent actor and should be on the stage. And the injury to his leg was real. Carrie could think of nothing worth deliberately wounding oneself to that extent. She had felt the complexity of Dan King from the first. Now she was more confused than ever.

Elsa came from the kitchen with the first platters of food and the next minutes completely occupied Carrie as she hurried between kitchen and dining room, keeping the food replenished and the coffee cups full.

She paid scant attention to Phil and Dan and only turned her thoughts in their direction when she heard a chair scrape. Looking up from the coffee she was pouring, she saw Phil stand. He motioned to her.

Now what does he want? Reluctantly, she walked down the opposite side of the table and stood behind Dan.

Phil walked around the table until he stood next to her. "I ain't gonna hurt you," he growled. "Need to talk with you private-like."

Wary, she asked, "How private?"

"Kitchen'll do, even if that old dragon will hear every word."

It couldn't be anything too personal if he was willing for Elsa to overhear, so Carrie consented.

Out of general earshot, Phil said, "Gotta be gone for a few days. King says he'll keep an eye on things at the Post for me."

Carrie's mouth dropped open. "You asked *Dan* to tend your store after he pulled a gun on you?"

"A man can forget a lot of things if he's got good reasons." A slow, secret smile hovered around the edges of his mouth and Carrie wondered what the "good" reasons might be.

"Besides," Phil added smoothly, "I need Dan's help." He advanced a step toward her. "Won't be any more trouble now that the man knows how it is between you and me."

Why wouldn't Phil take no for an answer? "There isn't *anything* between you and me," Carrie snapped. "Why do you keep insisting there is?"

Phil waved away her question. "Can't be holdin' a grudge against every man who falls for you. Jest have to feel sorry for his wasted yearnings. Besides, I figure I'll get more'n my fair share out of the bargain," Phil said with a smirk.

That's the first honest thing you've said recently, Carrie thought, but bit back any comment. Instead she said, "Dan can't do much of a job with that leg of his."

"Don't need him to do no heavy work. Willie can take care of that. But he's not bright enough to manage the business end. Got some shipments coming in. Need someone who can see to it I don't get cheated."

Carrie shook her head. She guessed she'd never understand men.

Then it occurred to her that Phil had been gone a great deal in recent weeks—far more than she could ever remember before. She knew his greed and need for power were insatiable. He *had* to be up to something.

"Mind telling me where you're going?" she asked, giving Phil a disarming smile.

"Just away. Nothing to bother your pretty little head over. Be back in two or three days. Give you some time to think about my proposal."

"It didn't sound much like a proposal. More like a threat," she retorted.

Phil's eyes lit up. "Soon as I get back, I'll have that ranch. Then I'll be over to ask for your hand in marriage, real proper-like."

"I didn't mean to give you any encouragement. The answer will be 'no' as always."

Carrie picked up a pot of hot coffee from the stove, sailed past Phil, and into the dining room. Her words never seemed to penetrate his massive ego, so further talk was useless. But she decided to reserve judgment on

Dan's working with Phil until he had an opportunity to explain.

Phil returned to the dining room too, stopped for a moment beside Dan, then hurried out the front door. Carrie could hear and almost feel his booted feet pound their determination into her front steps and across the dusty street.

The clatter of horses' hooves and the jangle of harness suddenly cut across the noise of the dining room, announcing the arrival of the stagecoach. Those still at the breakfast table hurried into the lobby to claim their bags and join the ones already waiting to take the stage south. All except Dan. He nursed a third cup of coffee as Carrie carried dirty dishes to the kitchen and reset the long table in preparation for feeding the stagecoach passengers.

Finding she had a moment to spare before the passengers filtered in for breakfast, Carrie slid into the chair next to Dan's.

"What brought you to the lobby so early this morning?" she asked.

"Came on Phil's invitation. He sent word last night he had some business to talk over. Wanted to meet me there before breakfast, he said."

"You saw the business he had in mind, didn't you?"

"I did."

"You're crazy, going to work for Phil!" she exclaimed. "You can barely stand on that leg."

"I'm the only available man in town right now. Besides, I don't have to do the heavy work, just supervise. I should be able to do that sitting down."

"If you're so short of money you have to work, you can earn your keep here at the hotel. I can always use help."

"I'm not so interested in the money as I am in getting inside Hardesty's operation. I know you don't trust him. And he doesn't set well with me, either. Nothing about him does . . . right down to his voice."

A passenger came into the dining room cutting short their discussion. The Army captain pulled off his hat and, standing in the archway to the lobby, beat out the dust that had settled in every wrinkle of his blue serge uniform. Choosing the place across from Dan, he pulled out the chair and sat down.

"Good place to eat?" he asked casually as Carrie filled his coffee cup.

Dan eyed him carefully. "The best."

"I could use some good home-cooking after Army chow."

"I know what you mean," Dan said, and laughed. "You coming from Montana Territory?"

The captain nodded.

"How do things look up north?" Dan asked.

"Not good. Indians are real restless. A lot of liquor's finding its way onto the reservation. And the ranchers are sick of the rustling. If something isn't done soon to diffuse the situation, things could get ugly."

Dan narrowed his eyes and slowly twirled a spoon. "How come you're going the other way from trouble, then?" he asked casually.

Carrie moved around the table serving the other coach passengers who'd followed the captain inside. After traveling all night, the people were so tired they ate quietly. There was little talk to cover what Dan and the captain were saying.

"Going to Cheyenne for reinforcements," the captain continued. "At least, I'm going to *try* to convince them we need help up here."

"Any idea who's behind it all?"

"Ideas, yes. Proof, no. And I can't get help based on suspicions. Fellows at headquarters like to follow channels all the way to Washington. Takes a long time to do it that way and it's easier than riding out and getting their uniforms dirty." He cast a rueful eye at his own dust-dimmed clothes.

The captain accepted the platter of ham and eggs being passed his way and, after filling his plate, ate hungrily. It was clear he wanted to eat, not talk.

Dan slid his chair back and reached for his crutch which was leaning against the wall. Carrie looked up from her work to see Dan motion her toward the kitchen. She held the door for him and he hobbled through.

"Mind sending me a sandwich for lunch?" he asked. "Don't think I'll get over if that freight order comes in."

"We'll see that you get fed."

Dan picked up a toothpick and lounged against the back door. "Sure would like to know where Phil's taking off to." He said it softly, as if he were talking to himself. Then, shaking off his reverie, he snapped the pick in half and slowly maneuvered himself outside.

Dan's comment stayed with Carrie as she finished the breakfast dishes and hurried to the wash house to set the water to heat. It was then that she noticed Phil hoist himself into his buckboard and drive slowly north out of town.

The sudden thought struck her that if she followed him, she could tell Dan where Phil had gone. She would have to wait, though, and hope she could track him. The terrain was too flat for her to follow close behind him. He'd spot her for sure.

While the water heated, Carrie went back into the hotel to help Elsa start lunch.

"Most of our crowd left on the stage so we're not going to be very busy," Carrie said easily as the two women worked side by side in the kitchen. "Think I'll go for a little ride after dinner."

"In this heat! You've lost all your senses!" Elsa exclaimed. "What you need is a nap."

Carrie laughed. "Not really. I can sleep this winter." If she kept her voice light, Elsa would be much less suspicious. It wasn't easy to fool her and the last thing Carrie wanted was an argument.

It was mid-afternoon before Carrie could get away without causing undue concern. She walked leisurely down the street to the livery stable where she kept her horses. No one was about so she chose a chestnut gelding, quickly saddled him, and led him outside. Swinging expertly into the saddle, Carrie turned onto the road going north. There were two sets of fresh tracks, one set made by the stagecoach, and the other by a team and buckboard. At the top of a short climb where the road rose out of the creek bottom, it forked. The buckboard had taken the fork leading toward the Indian reservation.

Chapter 5

Once Carrie picked up the wagon tracks, she rode along paying little attention. Phil wasn't likely to turn off anywhere. Though the day was hot, the land, cooled by the never-ceasing wind, lay before her in undulating waves of lush grass. As she drew closer to the timbered hills at the foot of the Owl Mountains—the high, rugged peaks still snowcapped in August—sleek cattle grazed and fattened on the limitless feed of the open range. The agency was located in the foothills, and further into the Owl Mountains lay the huge Shoshone reservation.

Dust clouds ahead indicated a wagon coming toward her. Quickly, she took careful notice of the peculiarities of Phil's wagon and horse tracks. The approaching vehicle would distort them and give her a challenge.

When the Bensons had first come to Wyoming, Carrie had learned the art of tracking from an old Shoshone buck named Running Bear. Her father had found him wounded and deserted, and her mother had nursed him back to health.

Angry at those who had left him to die and grateful to his benefactors, Running Bear had stayed in Parke's Crossing and helped at the hotel as he was able. From Running Bear, she had also learned the essentials of the Shoshone language. But Carrie had kept these skills carefully hidden.

The wagon came abreast of Carrie and she waved her peaceful intentions. Two Indian men, Shoshones with dark eyes set between flat noses, stared unemotionally at her. Even though they were shaded by feather-decorated flat brims extending from black high-crowned hats, their copper-colored faces glistened in the heat of the day. It still startled Carrie to see Indians dressed in white man's clothes—dark twill or cast-off army trousers and flannel shirts in bright plaids.

Their wives and several children sat in the bed of the wagon, khaki government blankets wrapped around their shoulders. None gave Carrie any sign they recognized her, yet she was sure they had. Though she had never formally met them, the two families looked familiar to her. Their wagon rattled on past and Carrie watched the trail of dust as they continued on their way to Parke's Crossing for supplies at Phil's trading post.

Picking up Phil's partially obliterated tracks again, Carrie followed them until they veered off the main road. Here they made a new path toward the hills and thick forests of ponderosa pines and douglas firs. The faint trail angled to the north across the open grassland then sloped back into the trees. The ground was broken now by ravines, and at the bottom of the first deep one Carrie spotted Phil's buckboard. The ground was trampled by several horses, horses apparently ridden by men waiting for Phil's arrival.

Leaning far out of the saddle, Carrie studied the tracks intently. Each horse made a distinctive set of prints but one set interested her more than the rest. Phil had unhitched his wagon horse and ridden it away. This horse was shod with light shoes worn on the outside at the frog. That meant the horse had been ridden a considerable distance in the mountains.

Strange way to use a wagon horse. Might explain where Phil had been spending his time, however, Carrie mused.

An undisguised trail led upward into the trees. As Carrie gained elevation, she looked back at the wide sweep of rolling grass at her feet. A surge of love for the land swept through her. No wonder men came here to settle and make their fortunes. There was feed and water for as many cattle as a man could raise, and timber for fuel, buildings and fences.

Carrie caught a movement out of the corner of her eye as her gaze swept the wide panorama. She pretended not to notice and purposely turned away from it. Perhaps it was only a deer or a stray steer, but if it was a horseman, she was safer if he thought his presence had gone unnoticed.

As soon as she reached the cover of trees, she reined up and tied her horse. Taking field glasses from her saddle bag, she walked back to the tree line, taking care to remain concealed. Focusing the glasses, she peered into the ravine where she had detected the movement. Slowly she traced the ravine. Nothing!

She waited a moment, then tried again. This time she brought the magnified field upslope, closer to where she remained hidden. This sweep revealed a dark hat. It appeared to move of its own accord through the tall grass, a disembodied object bobbing slightly as it came toward the trees where she stood.

Carrie lowered the glasses and licked suddenly dry lips. There was a horse and rider below her, concealed by the ravine. *Indian?* she wondered. *Cowhand? Obviously somebody following me.*

Had they been waiting for her? Or was this a lookout placed by Phil and his party with instructions to follow anyone who intruded? That seemed the most reasonable explanation since no one except Elsa knew she had planned to ride out today.

Carrie decided to move on to put more distance between herself and the black-hatted rider. She followed a game trail filled with the hoof prints of Phil's party. The trail led through the pines and stands of thick firs as it wove its way upward to the crest of the ridge. She stopped often to listen but all that broke the stillness were the calls of birds and an occasional whisper of wind through the pine boughs. Her progress was slow and when she topped the forested crest of the first hill, the sun was casting long shadows across the narrow valley below.

Scanning the scene again with her field glasses, she found a dim trail cutting through the valley. Now, she had to make a decision. Should she continue her quest or give it up? If she turned back she was sure to meet the person tracking her. Would he believe her story about just being out for a ride? Whether Indian or white, if she didn't convince him, she could be in serious trouble. Carrie knew she wasn't a good liar, so it seemed in her best interests to continue.

She dropped down into the valley, riding along a winding trail well-marked by six horses which had passed earlier. Though she hadn't explored this particular area of the country before, she knew the boundaries of the reservation well enough to know she was close.

During the next three-quarters of an hour, Carrie carefully watched her back trail. Though she saw nothing and heard nothing, the birds quieted and she couldn't free herself from the sensation of being followed.

In the soft ground she saw deer and elk tracks mingled with the tracks of shod horses. Tracking here was no challenge and Carrie began thinking of ways to determine if she was, indeed, being followed.

She saw a break in the forest ahead and a patch of placid blue sparkling in the sunshine. Reining up on the edge of the meadow, Carrie savored the scene—a small lily-pad shaped lake set amid high grass and late-blooming wildflowers.

The tracks Carrie followed skirted the meadow, keeping close to the trees, but she needed a rest. Riding out to the water's edge, she dismounted. Her horse drank noisily through the bit and she stretched. The ground here was covered with the tracks of deer, elk and cattle, as well as the smaller, fainter prints of birds and small animals. This was obviously a common watering place for all the creatures of the wild.

Carrie looked back along the trail she had just covered. Her spine tingled and the hair rose on the back of her neck. She was definitely being watched—and by more than one pair of eyes!

Dear Lord, please help a foolish lady. I know I have no right to ask since it was my own doing that got me here, but you know I came with the best of intentions. Before mounting her horse again, she flipped the stirrup up onto the saddle horn and checked the cinch. That was when she saw the Indians.

Half a dozen Shoshone warriors, mounted like statues

on spotted ponies, stared at Carrie from inside the shadows of the trees crowding the edge of the meadow. The uneasy sensation of being followed hadn't been caused by the lone rider in the ravine, but by these warriors who had probably been at close range her entire trip.

The young men wore leather headbands festooned with a variety of feathers. Several carried old rifles, while others had revolvers and knives stuffed into the belts of their dirty buckskins.

As if by some unspoken signal, the warriors dug their moccasins into the horses' flanks and suddenly rode away into the trees. Carrie watched them disappear as silently as they had arrived, leaving the shadows undisturbed once again.

Carrie thought about turning toward Parke's Crossing and home, but she knew if she did, she would lose track of Phil and not know what he was up to until it was too late. Too late for what, she didn't know; it was just a foreboding she shared with Dan. Having made her choice to go on, she mounted and rode from the meadow, following a creek which meandered out of the lake.

She looked up once more at the high snowy peaks of the Owl Mountains. Those snow fields and glaciers birthed the streams that flowed into the valley below, providing a reliable source of water year round for animals and man. The water in the creek, gurgling and splashing its way over a bed of coarse sand and rounded granite rocks, flowed clear and sparkling as her mother's diamond.

Unexpectedly, the trail took an abrupt turn upwards and the climb became steep and winding. Carrie and her horse rose rapidly above the valley, leaving the thick-trunked trees behind. The trail blended into a talus slope and Carrie had to employ her finest tracking skills.

Dismounting, she eased her way over the rough rocks, giving her pony plenty of rein to do the same. An occasional telltale streak of white rock dust from the shoes of the horses she was following was all she had to go on. Once across the talus, the trail continued upward to another ridge. Now, Carrie faced a gravelly hillside descent. The horses she trailed had slipped frequently, leaving long furrows in the gravel. At the bottom, the loose rock gave way to dirt and here the tracks split.

The horse with the worn shoes and one other had begun a steep winding climb into the high country. The others had continued along the stream bed. To follow Phil, Carrie urged her mount up the steep hillside.

About half-way up, she had to cross another talus slope. But when she came out on the other side, she couldn't find the tracks. Tying her horse, Carrie walked back over the rocky hillside, keeping careful watch for white scratches in the earth. She found nothing. Though she crisscrossed the slide several times, she could not find the trail.

Engrossed in her tracking, Carrie failed to notice the sun slipping from view behind the tall mountain peaks. When she finally looked up, long golden rays were arching into the sky above the silver halo of light surrounding the peaks.

"Carrie, you haven't used much sense in your little expedition today," she said aloud, hoping the sound of her voice would calm the irregular thumping of her heart. "You'll never make it home before dark."

She had come ill-prepared to spend a night. Setting aside her fruitless search for the tracks of Phil's horse, Carrie clambered off the rocks and onto her pony. She needed shelter. This far north there was a long afterglow which she hoped would give her enough light to find a place out of the cold wind and heavy dew.

The evening breeze was already rising as the canyons began exchanging warm air from the grasslands for that cooled by the snow in the highlands. The flow brushed Carrie's warm cheek and she shivered slightly. Quickly, she turned the horse toward the cliffs towering above her. The crevices and shallow caves along the face would be ideal for protection. The ascent quickly became difficult, however, because the rock sloughing off the cliffs created an unstable walking surface. For Carrie's own safety and that of her horse, she dismounted and led him.

As she came closer to the cliffs, though, she again felt eyes watching her every movement. Surely the Indians hadn't ridden all the way up here. She was inside the forbidden sacred ground. But if it wasn't the Indians, then it must be Phil! Carrie grew sick at the thought, remembering his veiled suggestions of that morning.

Carrie walked along the shelf that ran in front of the cliffs, looking for a suitable shelter. As she walked around a protruding rock, she found a small spring flowing directly from the mountain. It cascaded in a tiny falls over the rocks, giving life to mosses and tender green plants. At its base, the frothy miniature falls splashed into a small pool. Carrie drank deeply and then watered her horse. Suddenly, she could *feel* a pair of eyes staring at her. They seemed to be in front of her and very close. Pretending to check her saddle, she positioned the horse so she could look over him at the different openings along the cliff.

A slight flash of white in the nearest cave caught her attention. Pretending not to notice, she continued to tighten, then loosen the cinch—anything to buy time as she tried to learn who or what watched her with such intensity.

There it was again—that slight flash of white. Leaving her horse to graze on the grass which surrounded the pool, Carrie walked slowly toward the opening.

She stopped about ten feet away. "Come out of there," she demanded, authority ringing in her voice. While she knew she must act unafraid, she had no intention of going any closer.

"Hurry up. Get out here!" She crossed her arms and tapped her foot impatiently.

In the dim light she saw the white flash again, then a small body became visible. Two wide, frightened eyes set in a round flat face peered at her from under a headband of leather decorated with white feathers. Carrie wanted to laugh and cry at the same time. Speaking to the little boy in Shoshone, she assured him she was a friend and that she would like to stay the night with him.

"Are you lost?" she asked, watching the little chin tremble as he attempted to control the tears which threatened to overflow.

"I Piube, Chief Washakie's son. Chief's son don't get lost. I just need daylight to find lodge."

"Of course that's all you need," Carrie said and held out her arms. The little fellow, probably not more than five years old, curled against her.

"It's too late tonight, but in the morning you can find the way and take me to your tent."

He sighed and wiped the tears with dirt-smudged hands. Carrie stifled the laugh at the cheeks that now looked like an imitation of his father's, painted for war.

Moving into the cave with him, Carrie shared the small amount of elk jerky she had with her and then worked to soften the rocky floor of the cave into a reasonably comfortable bed of tree boughs.

By the time the night birds began their song and the

moon had risen to dim the early stars, Carrie and little chief Piube were curled together on the fragrant bed. Carrie covered them with the blanket she had thoughtfully tied behind her saddle.

"You sleep. I keep watch," Piube said manfully.

"If you say so," Carrie agreed. "Just so long as you keep watch lying next to me."

"If that gives you peace," he replied with great seriousness.

"It does," Carrie said, glad his back was to her so he couldn't see the smile she couldn't control.

In a very short time, heavy breathing told her the exhausted little boy was fast asleep. Probably the first restful sleep he'd had since he became lost, Carrie thought before sleep overcame her, too.

Chapter 6

In the morning, with little Piube by her side, Carrie stood in the mouth of the shallow cave and gave thanks for the protection given during the night. She looked out over the wild country first seen by white men when a teenaged Shoshone, Sacagawea, led them west.

Carrie never ceased to be stirred by the majestic beauty of this land. Calls of many birds challenged the rushing sounds of clear water. The air was pungent with the fresh smell of vegetation—variegated shades of green in spring and summer, turning in fall to brilliant hues of red, orange and yellow. With their deep unchanging green, the firs and pines stabilized the landscape and gave it permanence. Over all, granite peaks stood guard; their strength undiminished by time; their dominion unshaken by man.

These were the sacred mountains of the Shoshone.

According to the story Running Bear had told her, the Crow and Shoshone chiefs had journeyed alone deep into the mountains. There they met in a secret place and engaged in mortal combat. The battle was long and bloody as each strong warrior repeatedly wounded the other. But at sundown the bloodied Shoshone chieftain stood over his foe, and in one final act of triumph cut the heart from his fallen enemy's breast.

Only on certain occasions, with permission of the medicine men, did Shoshone tribesmen venture into the sacred mountains. No white man was ever permitted to travel into these remote valleys and canyons.

Carrie looked down at the sturdy little warrior and wondered what would happen to them both when it was learned they had been on forbidden ground. However, she made no mention of her concerns to him.

"I believe I saw some ripe berries not far from here," she said. "How does that sound for breakfast?"

He sighed. "I have eaten much berries. I would like meat."

"If we take time to trap some meat, we will be too long returning to your home. Berries will get you back to your mother and father much faster."

"I will be a failure if I return from my hunting trip without meat." His eyes, black points in a dirt-smeared copper face, glistened unnaturally.

"If that is your only problem," Carrie said, "I have dried elk strips in my saddlebag. If we eat berries, we can return with the meat for the tribe."

Piube nodded with great seriousness. "Thank you, white sister."

Carrie saddled her horse and sat Piube up in the saddle. The trail was too steep to ride down, so she walked and led the horse. It hurt to give up tracking Phil, but getting this little boy back to his tribe was more important. At least, she could tell Dan where Phil had gone. Not that his traveling into the forbidden mountains made any sense. The Shoshone penalty for trespassers was torture. His reasons must be overwhelming to risk death.

They stopped along the trail for a quick breakfast of berries and a long drink of water so cold it made the top of Carrie's head ache. Then Carrie mounted her pony and put Piube behind her. They moved through scanty bushes until they came to the game trail that had brought Carrie onto Piube's mountain. Carrie chose to skirt the small meadow where she had seen the Indians and traveled up the forested slope of the hill to the west. Her horse labored through the pine forests and dense stands of fir trees.

"Tell me, Piube," Carrie said, breaking the long silence, "why did you run away?"

"I didn't run away!"

She turned and looked into a face made furious by her accusation. "Then, why were you so far from the tribe?"

"Because my people are hungry and it is the chief's duty to see they are not. I am his son. It is my duty, too. I tried to find an elk. I followed the tracks. When I got tired, I rested. When I unrested, I saw the elk. I hunted him very well, but he did not want to feed my people. He ran far from me. Without a horse I could not keep up with him."

"But why are your people hungry? They are given plenty of beef by the government."

"No beef."

"Piube, only last week a big herd went past Parke's Crossing on its way to the reservation. There was enough meat to feed all your people for weeks—and feed them well."

"We don't have any meat," he insisted stubbornly. "I

followed the elk tracks into the mountains. I was only resting for the night when you came and scared the elk away." He was silent for some time. "We should go back and kill the elk."

"We don't have anything to kill it with, Piube."

"I can make a bow while you sharpen some arrows."

"I'm sure you could make a fine bow, but my arrow-sharpening ability isn't the best. I doubt I could satisfy you with my work."

"Useless squaw," he sniffed.

"Perhaps if you tell the other warriors what you found, you could lead them to the elk." Carrie hoped that would placate him. He was certainly being raised to be a good Shoshone chief.

"I can lead them right to the elk," he bragged.

Now Carrie knew what the warriors were doing at the meadow when she had stopped yesterday, and why they had left her unchallenged. The search for this child had undoubtedly occupied the entire tribe.

"How long have you been hunting your elk?" she asked.

"Four suns."

"Piube, you've been gone from your mother four days?"

Piube nodded. "Uh-huh."

His parents must be frantic, Carrie thought.

At a spring deep in the hills, Carrie stopped to rest and water the horse. She took careful note of the tracks of unshod ponies. They were fresh, covering those of the wild animals, meaning the Shoshones had been here this morning.

"Anything look familiar yet?" she asked Piube.

He squinted his eyes and with great seriousness looked carefully about. "Not too far from home now. Go that way."

He pointed west through the trees.

It was past noon when Carrie saw through the trees ahead to open ground. The basin, a stretch of nearly flat land rich with grass and wildflowers, extended across to the steep slopes of the Owl Mountains. The thick growth of brush indicated that a stream wound through this heartland of the Shoshones.

Though she rode with Piube, Carrie thought it best to stay in the trees. She didn't want to alarm the Indians. Slowly, they rode along the edge of the basin. Presently the land rose and they rode up a forested slope. It dropped sharply on the other side and Carrie sent the horse in a zigzag pattern across the face of the hill.

Carrie caught a whiff of wood smoke. Piube tightened his grip around her.

"We're almost home," he said. She turned to look at him and caught him wiping at unwanted tears.

As they broke from the trees, Carrie had a commanding view of the basin. Shrieks of children at play grew more strident and the dogs, excited by the children's activity, barked louder.

A haze of smoke hung in the windless air over the Shoshone village stretched across the grassy meadow below. More than two hundred lodges bunched along the meandering creek and women were working everywhere. The children's play was also work, as they watched the herds of spotted ponies. When one wandered away from the herd and headed for the trees, a child would quickly dash after it. All but the cradled infants were busy.

Carrie dismounted and reached for her field glasses. "I think we'd better be sure what's going on," she said to Piube. "With things as unsettled as they are, your people might think I have you as a hostage, shoot first and ask questions after."

"They would not do that," Piube assured her.

"Nevertheless . . . " Through her field glasses Carrie brought the activities into focus. Older women and little girls tended fires where large iron pots steamed. The younger women and older girls scraped deer and elk hides, stretched tight by wooden pegs driven into the ground. Carrie knew this was the first step in the tanning process to make a soft leather for clothing.

"I can see?" Piube asked and reached a tentative hand toward the glasses.

As Carrie handed them to him she spotted a hunting party emerging from the pines at the far edge of the meadow.

"Here, Piube. Look and tell me who's coming."

Piube could barely get his pudgy hands around the glasses and Carrie had to help him fit them to his eyes.

"It's my father right in front of me!" Piube exclaimed. He kept looking away and then back through the glasses, enchanted and mystified by the magnification. "They bring deer to feed my people."

Carrie took back the glasses and focused on the deer carcasses slung over some of the hunters' horses. There was a pitifully small amount of meat for the number of hungry people waiting to be fed. As the hunters drew near the village, children whooped and ran through the high grass to greet the party.

Carrie passed the field glasses back to Piube. He looked again and pointed to a tall, square-shouldered man in the lead.

"Washakie, chief. My father," he said, handing the binoculars back.

Carrie studied the chief through her glasses. The distance was too great to see the fine details of his face, but he rode proudly and regally. He wore buckskin trousers, and in his right hand he carried a rare prize among the Indians—a lever-action repeating rifle.

As the hunters approached the encampment, women and more children gathered around the men, laughing and chattering with excitement. Lifting the carcasses from the horses, the women began quickly skinning and preparing the meat. Soon, the tougher cuts and scraps bubbled in the pots and the rest turned on spits over hot coals.

It was nearly sundown before Carrie decided it was safe to ride into the camp. She and Piube mounted, but she placed him in front of her in the saddle.

"Smile and look happy," she coached. "I don't want your father to think I am coming with you as a prisoner."

"They know I would not sit quietly if you not a good person," Piube said seriously. "I would give cry of danger. Warn my people."

Piube directed Carrie to backtrack through the forest as they left their place of concealment in the pines. After about a quarter of a mile, they came to a trail which led directly into the open basin.

"From here my father can see us. Give them plenty warning and see you bring me back safe."

Angling out into the basin, they rode some distance through the belly-high grass. As Carrie neared the lodges, a warning shout went up, and running figures dashed for their horses.

Moments later a half-dozen mounted warriors armed with rifles, revolvers, and war clubs galloped toward Carrie and Piube. Carrie reined her horse to a stop and waited as the charging warriors drew close.

Piube waved and shouted a greeting. The Shoshone warriors swept past and around, encircling Carrie with their ponies. They shook their weapons at her as they milled about.

"Piube, they think I kidnapped you! Talk to them and tell them what happened or I'm going to be a dead woman."

Piube shouted in Shoshone too rapid for Carrie to understand. One of the warriors drew close, reached out, and touched Carrie's face. Carrie forced herself to smile, but there was no friendly response.

They do think I took Piube, she thought. *I'm going to be killed before I can explain.* Her heart thudded in her ears until she had difficulty hearing. Dying wasn't something she had prepared herself for today.

"Come!" Piube ordered. "We go to my father. He will believe me."

Carrie's heart sank. That meant Piube hadn't convinced the warriors. She urged her horse forward through the group of Indians who had formed a corridor to escort her toward the tall man waiting at the opening of the encircled lodges. Children ran and stood around the edge of the circle with their mothers and old men. One woman stood apart, her eyes glued to Piube. *His mother,* Carrie decided.

She was close enough now to see that Washakie was a handsome man. His nose, face, and chin were refined and sharper than the wide, flat features of most of his fellow tribesmen. In the crook of his arm, he carried the repeating rifle Carrie had seen through the field glasses.

He motioned to her and she dismounted. Safely on the ground, she reached out to help Piube when she felt cold steel across her arms. She felt the pressure of the rifle forcing her back.

Strong arms took Piube from the saddle and carried him to stand before his father. In a deep, powerful voice,

Washakie spoke to his son, "We have searched four suns and moons for you. Today we gave up and hunted to feed the people. People hungry because of you. Did this woman steal you?"

Piube vigorously shook his head. "She lost and came to my cave where I wait to kill big elk to feed my people. She scare away elk, but she say she has dried meat in her saddlebag."

"You were not lost?"

Piube looked at his father with great disgust. "No! I was hunting. I followed a great elk."

"You are too young to hunt."

"I am chief's son. I must help feed my people when they grow hungry."

Washakie shifted the Winchester and held it across his waist.

"I see," he said softly. Taking Piube by the hand, Washakie looked at Carrie, who was still surrounded by bristling weaponry, and said, "Come."

Carrie wanted to drop in her tracks. She had not been able to follow all of the rapid Shoshone exchange. She did not know what terrible torture he might be devising for her.

The crowd of Shoshone men, women, and children parted and the chief led the way toward one of the conical lodges built of lodgepole pine logs. It was straight and slender. The frame, covered with animal hides, had a small opening at the base for an entrance. Drawings of armed men pursuing animals decorated the lower part of the lodge and, rising above them, was a large red circle—the sun.

Sending Piube inside first, Washakie ducked to enter the teepee. Dropping the skin over the opening, Washakie left Carrie standing outside the lodge in the midst of several warriors. The silence was tense, broken only by Piube's childish voice and indistinguishable words. Suddenly, the flap snapped open and Washakie motioned Carrie inside. Unsure of his intentions, she hesitated and a sharp jab in the middle of the back reminded her that she had little choice.

Smells of leather and smoke tainted the air, nearly overwhelming Carrie as she and one guard entered the lodge. Unable to see clearly in the dim light, she felt her booted feet sink into something soft. Forced to her knees before the chief, she realized the floor was covered with a bear skin.

Cross-legged, Washakie, with Piube at his side, sat in front of Carrie.

"Now *you* tell story," Washakie ordered in broken English.

Carrie fought to keep the rising terror under control as she tried to decide if she should speak in Shoshone or English. A sharp kick on her thigh reminded Carrie she had better speak up and be quick about it. Her Shoshone was probably in the same elementary stage as his English, but Washakie would be more comfortable in his own language. It might make the difference whether she made it out alive. Briefly, she told her story.

Washakie listened intently but it was impossible in the dim light to read any message in his eyes or face. Piube's face, however, revealed his delight at her explanation for his being gone from the tribe—hunting for meat. She was sure that was what he had told his father. She made no mention that he was lost.

Washakie placed an affectionate hand on Piube. "You tell the same story as my son. I believe you."

Carrie expelled her breath before she realized she had been holding it.

"Thank you, Washakie and thank you, Piube." She nodded at them. "Tell me one thing, will you? Why are your people hungry? A large herd of cattle was delivered to the reservation last week. I know; I saw the herd as it passed through the basin, and the drovers who stayed at my hotel on their way back to Texas told me they left them for your people."

Washakie's eyes narrowed ever so slightly, the only indication of his feelings. "None came here. Have only had beef once since winter."

"That's not possible!" Carrie objected. "I've seen several herds go north and the drovers return to wash the trail dust off at my place. If you're not getting the beef intended for you, where is it going?"

"I don't know," he said, "but maybe I ought to find out."

"The man I was tracking yesterday rode into the Owl Mountains. Do you suppose they are holding the herds of cattle there?"

"Why would they do that?"

"If I had the answer, I wouldn't be sitting here puzzling it over with you," Carrie said bluntly. Then, before her courage died, she asked, "Do your young warriors gather courage to take scalps?"

"A few are making noises. No man likes to hunt and hunt and find little meat. It is painful to see his family hungry because he is unable to provide as he should."

Carrie nodded her understanding. Washakie rose gracefully and effortlessly to his feet and Piube scrambled to stand next to his father.

"Let her have freedom to go where she will," Washakie instructed those guarding her. "She has returned Piube safely to me. She can be trusted."

"Thank you, Washakie. I will not abuse your hospitality."

Carrie shared the evening meal with the Indians, but though it was delicious and she was famished, she ate little. Knowing she took food from the mouths of hungry children did much to deaden her appetite. Later, as a guest of Washakie, she spent the night in his lodge, giving him all but one piece of her remaining elk jerky as a gift.

Rising early the next morning, she slipped quietly from the teepee and hoped she didn't wake the still-sleeping family. It was probably the first good night's rest they had had since Piube's disappearance.

The only people stirring were the women building the fires. Carrie nodded at them and smiled as she hurried through the dew-covered grass to where her horse was tethered. It took only minutes for her to saddle up and ride slowly from the peaceful camp.

As she traveled, she gnawed on her remaining strip of jerky and pondered Washakie's words. Her trip had produced no answers and raised many more questions. Before returning to Parke's Crossing, Carrie decided, she would pay Jed Skyler a visit. If he didn't know where those cattle were, then he'd better start finding out.

Chapter 7

Dan unlocked the door to the trading post and swung it open. His leg throbbed from the exertion of walking from Carrie's hotel. He paused in the doorway to catch his breath and let the pain subside. Carrie hadn't returned last night either and the leg had gone untreated. He couldn't bring himself to pour that fiery liniment on it. And after the tongue-lashing Elsa had given him at two o'clock in the morning when she'd checked Carrie's room and found it still empty, he would let his leg rot before he'd ask Elsa for help.

He couldn't imagine where Carrie had gone or why. It didn't seem to fit her character to go riding idly off when there was so much work to do. If he could mount a horse, he'd be after her. But if he could mount a horse, he wouldn't be here at all. He'd be tracking Phil Hardesty. That man was up to no good and Dan would bet he was the cause behind the Indian unrest. For the hundreth time Dan wished he could place that voice. He *knew* he had heard it before.

Dan's pause in the doorway allowed the early morning air to circulate inside, hopefully diluting the cigar and pipe smoke still rank from last night's poker game in the bar.

Counters ran along either side of the store's one huge room and long tables filled the middle. Dan limped down the aisle along the hardware side where lanterns, harnesses, and pots hung from the ceiling, cobwebs stringing the items together like a mismatched necklace. Kegs of bolts and nails cluttered the floor and functioned as chairs for each new group of customers who came to visit in addition to making purchases.

If this was my store, Dan thought, *I'd sure clean things up. It's such a pigpen I doubt that Phil knows what he's got.*

Dan stared at the tables piled high with clothes, strewn and tumbled from careless hands and left unstraightened for months, or so it looked. Yesterday, after he'd taken care of the immediate problems, like sorting out sprouting potatoes and dumping weevilly flour, he'd started to bring some order to these tables. Today he hoped he could finish. If he forced himself to stay busy, maybe he could keep his mind off Carrie.

He crossed between the tables to the counter that served the grocery side. Here he stopped again and slouched on a high stool, giving his leg another rest.

Wretched thing! Going to keep me pinned down longer than I thought, he grumbled to himself.

A rasping sound made Dan look toward the rear of the building. The wide door into the saloon opened and Willie stepped into the store.

"Mornin'," he said, wincing unconsciously as he waited to see if Dan thought so, too.

"It definitely is morning," Dan said easily, trying to kid himself into believing everything was all right. "I hope it's a good one as well."

"Never can tell with Mr. Hardesty. Sometimes mornin's good and sometimes it's got here against his will. Them's the days I make myself real scarce."

Willie relaxed against the railing that separated Phil's desk and safe from the rest of the room. "Hear Miss Carrie's not come back from her ride yet. Seems a strange thing for her to do. Not like her at all. Not at all."

The bald crown of his head bobbed up and down as he talked, and pale eyes, set too close to his nose, squinted at Dan.

Dan tried to ignore Willie's last remarks. "Quite a party you had going last night," he said. "Usually that busy on a week night?"

"No. Funny thing, too. Never saw any of them boys before. Rode in for some fun, then left. Real closed-mouthed about their business." Willie's teeth clicked together inside his chinless jaws and he rubbed his hand over the shining pate as he talked. "Well, guess I'd better get the place cleaned up."

Dan nodded and turned his attention to the first customer of the day who was just entering the store.

"Hear Miss Carrie's not back yet," the woman said. "We're all getting mighty concerned, what with the Indians threatening to ride off the reservation."

Dan stood silent, watching as the woman chose her supplies and laid them on the counter. He didn't want to think about what might be happening to Carrie because he was helpless to do anything about it. He knew two nights was a long time in this country for a woman alone.

83

The woman stuffed her few items in the sack she'd brought, paid for them and, without further conversation, left.

Dan's day did not improve. Everyone who came into the store or passed through on the way to the bar commented on Carrie's absence. Nobody, however, volunteered to ride out to look for her. By evening, Dan's leg burned with an unquenchable fire, and his disposition matched it. Willie stuck his head through the door, took one look at Dan's face and, without a word, disappeared back into the bar.

Dan reproached himself for being so helpless as he limped his way to the saloon door. "I'm going to lock up now, Willie. Boys will be coming through the back door for the rest of the evening."

Willie, apparently unwilling to risk any more contact with Dan, merely nodded and went back to polishing the glasses. He stacked them on the ornate back bar where they reflected in the mirrored wall. It was plain to see the money was made here, and Phil's heart lay with it. He had spared no money to make the saloon one of the finest Dan had seen recently. From the long carved mahogany bar with its polished brass rail and spittoons, to the four round, green felt-covered tables with captains' chairs and kerosene overhead lamps, everything spelled money. A few regular customers wandered in and Dan left.

Without lighting the lamp in the wash house, he eased down onto the mattress and stretched out his aching leg. He hurt everywhere, and each time he thought of Carrie, he got sick to his stomach. Knowing he could do nothing for her, he became so angry at whoever had spooked his horse, he could taste the bile rising in his throat.

Dan had committed his life to Christ as a child and attempted to live according to Christ's teachings, but his faith was being sorely tried right now. *Lord, I can't endure the thought of Carrie out there alone. And I can't help her. This is the biggest test of faith you've sent my way since Anna, and I'm not passing it very well, I realize. Please keep Carrie safe and bring her home. Please, Lord,* Dan pleaded silently.

The door latch rattled and the hinges squeaked their rebellion at being moved.

"Dan, you in here?" Elsa asked, her tone much subdued from the early-morning harangue.

"I'm here," he answered, wondering what was in store for him now.

A match flared into life and Elsa lit the coal oil lamp. She didn't look directly at him but stood wiping her hands on her apron and shifting her eyes about the room.

"I owe you an apology for my behavior this morning," she said. "I had no right to take my worries out on you. You're not responsible . . . and you're hurt besides."

She pulled out a handkerchief and put it to her nose. "It's just . . . " she sniffed, "I don't know what to do about Miss Carrie. All the able-bodied men are out tending their ranches." Her shoulders shook as she broke into tears. "Not a soul to go help that poor girl."

Dan felt sorry for Elsa. She loved Carrie, that was abundantly clear. And here he lay, unable to help Carrie when she needed him. The thought galled him and turned him cranky.

"Nothing we can do tonight." His voice came out sharp and angry.

Elsa's head shot up and she turned confused eyes on him. Dan felt some remorse over being so abrupt but didn't bother to explain.

"If she isn't back by morning, we need to notify the Army and get them on a search," he continued.

85

"Sorry I troubled you." Now it was Elsa's turn to sound cross and irritated. "Thought somehow you might appreciate the good work Carrie did on you. See I was mistaken." She turned abruptly and started for the door.

Dan sat up. "Don't go, Elsa. I'm not upset at you. I'm angry that I can't sit a horse and go find Carrie myself. Angry that I'm a helpless cripple when I need to be my strongest."

Elsa stopped, then continued on outside, leaving the door ajar.

"Well, you've made a fine mess of things now," Dan muttered, scolding himself. "Don't know what more I could say, though. Guess Elsa doesn't understand how things are with me."

He lay back down and gave himself over to the pain stabbing through his leg and up into his hip. As Carrie had predicted, because he hadn't stayed off his leg it was getting worse, not better.

How long he lay staring at the peeling logs of the ceiling and brooding over the fate that had brought him here, Dan didn't know. Elsa's footsteps brought his thoughts back to the bare little room. She entered, carrying a tray laden with napkin-covered dishes.

"Can't have you starvin'." She set the tray on the stove and peered down at him. "You want me to fix your leg or you want to eat first?" she asked.

"I didn't think you did nursing."

"I don't usually. Carrie's so much better than me, I leave it up to her. I cook better."

"Leg hurts so bad tonight, anybody could work on it."

Silently, Elsa brought the kit from the shelf and set to work. Dan thought the top of his head would come off when she poured on the liniment; even through clenched teeth a groan escaped.

"Sorry, but you should have had that tended to this morning and at noon." Elsa lectured and bandaged at the same time. "You're going to end up with a bad infection if you don't take care of it."

When she finished, she set the supper tray by Dan and cleaned up the nursing mess. She didn't wait for him to finish eating.

"Just leave the tray. I'll fetch it in the morning. I didn't go to bed at all last night and I'm so tired I can hardly move. Won't sleep, but I'm going to lie down. I can at least rest."

Dan wished he had some words of comfort for Elsa, but anything he might say would sound insincere for they both knew that Carrie's chances of being found alive were dwindling with each passing hour.

"Take care, Elsa. Guess prayer is all we have to rely on tonight."

"Don't you worry. I've been doing plenty of that."

His leg felt better but he couldn't sleep. Every time he closed his eyes, Carrie's face appeared. Those big wide eyes, blue as a rain-freshened Wyoming sky, smiled at him, friendly and trusting. And he had failed her trust.

At last he could stand his thoughts no longer and, grabbing his crutch, he hobbled out into the cool night air. Cricket songs filled the darkness and the air over the basin hung unmoving, full of dust and smoke.

Dan hobbled out into the street and stopped. A lamp was lighted in the store. Carefully, he moved across the street until he could see through the dirt-streaked window. Inside, Phil leaned against the grocery counter, arms folded, watching a Shoshone squaw debating how to best spend her few coins spread on the counter.

When did Phil get back? Dan wondered. Strange he

87

would open the store for an Indian with so little money. He seemed in no hurry, either, but waited patiently for her to make up her mind. *Trip must have gone his way,* Dan thought.

Dan looked about for the wagon that had brought the Indian woman to town. But the street was empty. Dan limped toward the big loading platform in the back. Easing around the corner of the building, he heard the stomp of horses' hooves and the soft jingle of harness. In the moonlight it was easy to see the team and buckboard. *The bar's closed. So why is the wagon behind the store?* Dan pondered. If the squaw was grocery shopping, why wasn't the wagon tied in front?

Something bothered Dan. Keeping an eye on the back door, he pulled deeper into the shadows to watch and wait.

He didn't wait long. The door opened and Hardesty came out carrying two jugs. Only one thing in the store came in containers like that—whiskey! So Hardesty *was* the one selling the Indians whiskey! Two gallons in the stomachs of a dozen wild bucks could start a burning and killing raid that would sweep over the grassland like a wildfire. And Hardesty was willing to risk this for the twenty-five dollars the sale would bring him. The man was mad! He was so in love with money, he'd take any risk to accumulate more.

Dan's mouth curled in contempt. Parke's Crossing itself might be the target of a raid, and Phil the one killed. But greed had obviously blinded him to the risk.

With the whiskey safely hidden under a blanket in the back of the wagon, Hardesty returned inside and shut the door.

Well, this whiskey won't be delivered, Dan decided. He moved silently to the buckboard and lifted out the jugs.

With the crutch in one hand, it was impossible for him to carry both bottles at the same time. He stashed one under the steps and then, carrying the other in his free hand, he hobbled past the blacksmith's shop and corral to a stack of straw. There, he hid the first jug and hurried back to pick up the second.

He was in the shadow of the livery stable when the squaw came out. He prayed she would trust Hardesty enough not to check on the whiskey. If she checked and found it missing, she would demand replacement. Hopefully, having seen Phil take it out, she would just drive away. When she got back to the reservation and found the wagon empty, she would be back, Dan knew, but that wouldn't be until tomorrow.

The old squaw hoisted her fat body into the wagon seat and slapped the reins. The horses moved slowly and steadily off into the night.

Dan breathed a silent prayer. For now, at least, he had bought a little time.

Chapter 8

Carrie rode across the timbered foothills, never seeing the Indian warriors who followed her. But she sensed their silent escort and, on occasion, heard their ponies' hooves crunch against rocks on the downward trails. Since Washakie had seemed satisfied with her story last night, she wondered why the escort this morning. But she wasn't fearful.

It was late afternoon when Carrie broke out of the trees, and could see the agency house in the distance. She had gauged her position more accurately than she had dared hope. Urging her horse into a brisk canter, she soon arrived in the wagon yard. The place was deserted. Carrie felt little nips of fear dance through the hair at the back of her neck. This wasn't usual. A wagon or two and several horses always waited in the yard.

Quickly she dismounted and ran up the steps. She

could hear her knock on the wide pine door echo through the house and go unanswered. She rapped once more for good measure. Finally, from deep inside the house, Carrie heard the sound of shuffling feet, and after several long seconds, the housekeeper, Matwanda, opened the door just wide enough to see through. Carrie stared into sullen eyes.

"May I come in, please? I need to see Jed."

"Ain't here," came the terse reply, and she made no move to open the door further.

The woman was impossible. How Alice tolerated her, Carrie would never know. *I'd do without help before I'd put up with this peevish creature,* she thought.

"Then tell Alice I've come to visit," Carrie requested sharply, thoroughly vexed at being kept out on the porch.

"Ain't here, neither."

Carrie glared her displeasure, but the dumpy figure seemed rooted to the spot.

"Where is she?" Carrie demanded to know.

A loose-jointed shrug was the housekeeper's only answer.

"You do too know!" Carrie snapped, her eyes flashing a fire which was building rapidly inside.

"Mister sent her away. Big trouble on the reservation. Indians could attack any minute."

"If that's true, what are you doing here?"

Reaching for a ragged handkerchief, the pitiful soul covered a large sniff of despair.

"They don't care about me. I can get tortured or scalped and them two don't fret none. Serve 'em night an' day," she whined. "That's the pay I get. I'm nothin'. When I'm dead and gone, they'll hire another unsuspectin' body to wait on 'em."

Carrie regretted ever having asked. "So, where did Jed send Alice?"

"How should I know? He don't tell his business to me."

"Where did Jed go?"

"Thinks he knows it all, him havin' been in the Army and all. Gone out to settle the Indians' hash all by hisself. Lucky if he comes back with his hair, if he comes back at all."

Carrie suppressed her exasperation, extended her thanks and walked slowly to where her horse stood. Matwanda's story didn't fit the circumstances. There was no trouble brewing on the reservation of the dimensions she described. She had seen the majority of the tribe, and Washakie could handle the discontent among the hungry braves. These thoughts, coupled with worry over the distress she knew she had caused Elsa, kept Carrie's mind busy as she rode back to Parke's Crossing.

Arriving near supper time, the town looked normal for the time of day. The tie rails in front of the hotel and the saloon were full of dusty, lathered horses. Carrie brushed at the hordes of flies civilization attracted and hurried to the livery stable. Poor Elsa must be nearly swamped working the hotel alone.

"Evening, Zeb," she called as she led her horse into the dusky interior.

Zeb whirled and nearly lost his balance on his good leg. The other, mutilated by the War, served only to prop him up.

"Miss Carrie! Oh, praise the Lord!"

His southern accent hadn't diminished over the years, leaving no doubt as to which side of the War he had served.

"Whole town's been frettin' near out of their minds with

you gone. Thought for sure the Indians had you."

His young son rushed up from deep inside the building and took the reins of Carrie's horse.

"As a matter of fact, the Indians *did* have me," Carrie replied calmly.

"Land, don't tell Miss Elsa *that*! Poor woman's in such a state now she's not likely to recover. She finds that out, she's a goner for sure!"

"They treated me very well, but I am sorry to hear Elsa is in such a state."

Carrie turned to the little boy. "You take extra special care of my horse and I'll buy you a piece of horehound candy at the trading post."

"Yes, ma'am!" His eyes changed from wide-eyed excitement at her "escape" from the Indians, to sparkling with anticipation.

Carrie smiled as she remembered her own youthful delight over a horehound drop dissolving on her tongue and trickling its goodness down her throat. But this memory reminded her how hungry she was. The jerky had kept her stomach satisfied but her taste buds longed for some variety. Besides, she must see Elsa.

"Thanks, Zeb," Carrie called before she ran down the street to the hotel. Pulling off her riding gloves, Carrie dashed up the back steps. She burst into the kitchen wondering frantically what she would say to Elsa . . . the kitchen was empty! The fire had gone out and the cook stove sat like a shiny black monster controlling the kitchen by virtue of its size. The sounds of restless chairs scraping in the dining room told Carrie that hungry men wanting their supper had tired of waiting and were about to invade Elsa's sanctuary.

Carrie flew through the door to the dining room.

"I'm sorry but your supper's going to be late," she said

in a rush. "Elsa's not here and I only just got back."

"How long you figure it'll take?" The large man at the foot of the table stood and glared down at her.

Carrie ran her eyes up and down the full table of men staring coldly at her. Hungry men had no heart and could care less about Elsa's disappearance.

"If you don't mind sandwiches and no coffee, about fifteen minutes."

"That all right with you boys?"

The men nodded.

The floor clock struck six times as Carrie scurried back inside the kitchen and set to work. She grabbed loaves of fresh bread from the buttery and began slicing, thankful that Elsa had baked before...before what? Carrie suddenly realized only one thing could have kept Elsa from her work. She must be sick! Dreadfully sick! She wished she had a minute to find Elsa and tell her she was safe, but Carrie dared not risk the further wrath of her guests. She'd heard stories of how fine establishments had been turned into kindling for less reason than these men had.

The clock bonged 6:15 when she entered the dining room with heaping platters of roast beef sandwiches and pitchers of cold water. Conversation ceased as the food was rapidly passed around the table.

Carrie returned to the kitchen to make a second round of the husky sandwiches and slice berry pies. Bless Elsa! The pie would rescue the meal.

She placed the refilled platters on the table and set a piece of pie in front of each man. Exclamations of appreciation rose from the diners.

"Say, ain't you the little lady what was lost?" a gravelly voice asked.

Carrie had no wish to explain her trip or her disappear-

94

ance so she just nodded and continued about her business.

"Injuns get ya?" he pursued.

Now that plenty of food was on the table, Carrie ignored the question and hurried upstairs to Elsa's room. She knocked softly on the door in case Elsa was asleep. But a weak "come in" invited Carrie inside. She opened the door and felt the heat of the unventilated room.

Carrie tiptoed to the bedside. "Elsa, what's the matter, dear?"

Elsa rolled over and Carrie stared at the pinched features overwhelmed by great dark-circled eyes. Elsa's appearance frightened Carrie.

"Elsa, speak to me!" she commanded.

Surprise and confusion ripped apart the apathy as Elsa recognized Carrie. "I . . . I . . . I thought you were dead," she stammered. "Nobody's gone three days in an Indian scare and comes back alive."

Refusing to give in to her desire to weep over the grief her absence had caused, Carrie briskly straightened the covers and patted Elsa's pillow to fluffiness.

"I have," she said in a firm voice. One hint of weakness on Carrie's part and Elsa would dissolve into a flood of tears, and huggings and kissings. Carrie was not up to a demonstration of that sort.

"I'll bring you a sandwich and a glass of water. That's what the guests had."

Shock and relief edged Elsa's voice as she plucked with nervous fingers at the muslin sheet thrown over her legs.

"I'm sorry to let you down this way, but I . . . . " Her voice faded away and her eyes glistened with unshed tears.

"Don't worry. I'm here again and sorry I worried you. Your berry pie made up for the lack of variety at the dinner tonight, though. The men are full and content, but if I don't get back to register the rooms, they may not stay that way. I'll be up with your supper in a little while."

The next hour was busy and Carrie didn't have time to draw a free breath. But at last, with Elsa fed and overjoyed that Carrie was back, Carrie sat down among the scattered dirty dishes, finally able to satisfy her hunger with a sandwich and a piece of pie.

Looking back over the past four days, she felt she had lived a dream. Her well-ordered life had been shocked into complete upheaval, first with the arrival of Dan and then her escapade while tracking Phil. She didn't dwell on Dan—couldn't for fear he had gone and she would never see him again. It frightened her that she cared for him. She knew so little about him and wasn't even sure if what she knew was the truth.

Her reverie was interrupted by the opening of the back door. Since few people used that door, she wondered who it could be. She hoped it wasn't Phil. She wasn't ready to face him just yet.

Embarrassed to be caught wool-gathering, she quickly stuck a stack of dirty plates in the sink before turning to see who'd come in.

"Dan!" she exclaimed. The look on his face said he was equally surprised to see her. "You're still here!" She blushed at the surprised pleasure in her voice.

He gave a dry chuckle but his eyes held no mirth. "I probably wouldn't be if I could get on a horse."

He shut the door and limped into the room. "I'd be out trying to find a certain wandering citizen of Parke's Crossing. As it was, I had to send for the Army to do the job instead."

Reaching for the dishpan, Carrie's hand stopped in mid-air. "You what!"

"What were we supposed to do? Do you realize that

nobody has seen or heard from you since shortly after noon three days ago?"

His voice held a hard edge and, for the first time since he had come into the room, she looked carefully at him. His red-rimmed eyes showed lack of sleep and the lines on his face seemed taut and more finely drawn than she had remembered.

"Dan . . . I'm really sorry about not getting back. I had no intention of being away more than a couple of hours—maybe three. Let me get you something to eat and I'll tell you what happened."

Almost reluctantly Dan allowed himself to relax and listen to her adventures as he ate a piece of pie.

"Came back with a lot of loose ends, didn't you?" he said as she finished her story almost half an hour later.

"It's not much help, is it?" she apologized.

"Maybe there's more to what you learned than we know." Briefly Dan related the whiskey episode to Carrie.

"Since Phil's the one getting the liquor to the Indians, maybe he was making a delivery when you followed him."

"Then why were all those men waiting for him? The horses were shod so it wasn't Indians. I don't think he took liquor. Once they were in the mountains, they rode fast, like they had a specific destination to reach. I think they have something hidden in the Owl Mountains. That would be the safest place to keep something they don't want the Indians to know about, wouldn't it?"

She gathered up Dan's plate and water glass. "I'm most concerned about Alice. She isn't here in town, is she?"

"She hasn't come near the bar or I would have known. And she isn't here at the hotel unless she came this afternoon. Elsa indicated when I came over for dinner that she didn't have a single room rented."

"With Phil back, why are you still at the store?"

"I mentioned to him that the place was a mess. Says he isn't good at keeping things in order. I'm taking an inventory. He hired one of the older kids to count and I can sit to make the record. Might as well get paid for sitting. Besides, keeps me near him. He doesn't make a move I don't know about."

"Doesn't make any false moves, though, does he?"

"Only when he put the whiskey in the wagon. Been clean as a new pin ever since."

"I still think Alice's disappearance has something to do with all this. I intend to have a look in the morning."

"You, my dear lady, have had quite enough 'looks' on your own. I'll go with you, since I know it's useless to suggest you stay here."

"You're right about that. But how do you plan on going with me? A wagon's too slow and you can't ride a horse yet. Besides, you're supposed to work at the store."

"You'd be surprised what I can do. Give my leg a good doctoring tonight, and I'll be up and mounted before you."

Secretly, Carrie was delighted at the thought of Dan accompanying her, but she gave him no hint. It would never do to let him know how much he occupied her thoughts; how she enjoyed his company and hurt when they parted.

Carrie, you simply must get your head and heart together. You don't know his relationship with the Lord. In the west, talk comes cheap and fast, and he has given you nothing but words to go by. But in her heart she held firmly to the hope that he was truly a Christian.

Dan scraped his chair away from the table and, groping

for his crutch, stood up. "I'll be back when Phil closes the store. See you then."

Carrie put aside the weariness threatening to overwhelm her, built a fire to heat water, and cleaned up the supper dishes.

Finally finished for the evening, Carrie stepped through the back door and into the soft night air, brisk and refreshing after the heat of the day. She sank onto the porch stoop to watch the sky turn to deep purple and fill with stars. The lights in the trading post blinked out one by one until only the outline of the building loomed against the grassland beyond. The tall, snowy peaks of the Owl Mountains captured the last of the twilight and stood like spectres above the shape of the store.

Her thoughts turned again to Alice. *Where was she? What was happening to her?* Carrie closed her eyes to ask the Lord's help and protection for her friend, knowing that Alice in her troubled state desperately needed it.

Dan's slow limp roused her and he settled down on the step next to Carrie. They sat quietly, neither speaking. Carrie longed for him to take her hand and fold it in his. Maybe even gently kiss the tips. But though they sat side-by-side for a long time, he kept his distance, leaving her untouched.

As the night closed around them, Carrie suddenly didn't care if Dan owned a thing on this earth. It would be so comfortable to have someone to share her life with, be he drifter, rancher, or banker. Dan was fast winning her heart and only their being together mattered. She had possessions enough for both of them and Dan wasn't lazy. With his organizational abilities and desire to work, they could make a good life right here in Parke's Crossing. If only she knew where he stood with the Lord.

Chapter 9

Women in the town liked to help out at the hotel on occasion for the extra money, but washing wasn't one of their favorite things to do. So although Carrie enlisted some extra help in the wash room today, she still did the hot, heavy scrubbing, leaving the hanging up, folding, and storing to the others.

Dan was already gone when Carrie entered the wash house. She had offered him a room in the hotel, but he had declined. Said he was grateful not to have stairs to climb. But he had built a fire in the stove and the water was already hot. *Bless that man,* she thought. He had also taken over the treatment of his leg, even pouring on the liniment. He told her it strengthened a man's character if he could bear self-inflicted pain. Carrie smiled at the comment as she set out the wash tubs.

Dan came into the wash house just as she was beginning to wring the clothes. He took the handle from her hands and deftly cranked it while she fed the sheets into the rollers.

"Looks like you've helped with wash before," Carrie commented.

For a brief moment his eyes took on a faraway look, then he gave her a slow, sad smile and nodded. Carrie wondered what was behind it all, and was afraid she would never know him long enough or well enough for him to tell her.

She dipped her hand into the cloudy water and felt around the bottom of the tub. Finding nothing, she picked up a nearby towel and began drying her water-wrinkled hands.

"All done, thanks to you," she said, making her voice bright to counteract his solemn face.

"Want me to help you hang them?"

"No. I have help today, thanks." She took off the yellow oilcloth apron that protected her dress against sloshed water and hung it on a nail behind the door.

"You ready to go see about Alice?" His voice and face looked normal. He had apparently buried whatever caused the deep sadness.

"Yes, as soon as I change. Faded calico isn't in style this year for afternoon investigations. Are you ready?" She looked hard at him and then at his leg.

"Don't give this leg a second thought. I'll manage." He stepped behind Carrie and followed her out the door.

As they approached the stairs to the kitchen, he said, "Thought you might be interested to know Hardesty left a while ago. This time on horseback and in a big hurry. A couple of drifters wandered in and the three of them had a deep conversation at one of the game tables. Then Phil invited the boys to slake their thirst—at his expense—and he took off like a scared rabbit."

Carrie whirled about. "When did that happen?"

"Just before I came to the wash house."

"And you waited all this time to tell me? Why?" She pushed him aside and started toward the livery for her horse.

"Because I knew you'd react this way," he called after her. "You'd want to drop everything and dash after him."

"And what do you want to do? Give him enough lead so we can't find him? I'm beginning to think you're on his side in all this. That all your dislike is an act to draw suspicion away from you!"

The look on his face told her how wrong she was and she wanted to cut out her tongue. Slowly, she walked back to where he slumped against the stairs.

"I'm sorry," she said. "I had no call to speak to you like that."

He tipped his head and his hat covered his face. Silently, he climbed the steps and disappeared into the kitchen. Fighting back tears, Carrie followed him. He went into the dining room and Carrie dished up the meal and served them both. Elsa must have sensed the strain for she went about her work without speaking.

When Dan finished, he shoved back his chair and stood. "Meet me at the stream behind the hotel after you've changed. I'll have the horses." His voice was as impersonal as if he had been talking to a fence post.

Serves me right. Why I said such awful things to him, I'll never know. Carrie watched out the dining room window as Dan hobbled across the street to the corral.

Then dashing upstairs, she changed into a dark brown corduroy divided skirt, tan long-sleeved blouse, and a calf-skin vest. Slipping into scuffed, work-softened, high boots, she rushed downstairs and paused only long enough to let Elsa know she was going to see Alice.

"How many days you plannin' to be gone this time?" Elsa asked in a crisp voice devoid of all feeling.

She hasn't forgiven me yet for what I put her through the last time. "Not more'n two, maybe three. Dan's going with me." The only way to handle Elsa when she was like this was with sarcasm.

Elsa's jaw dropped and her face turned red, but she didn't say a word.

Smiling slightly at Elsa's expression, Carrie set her low-crowned tan Stetson on her head and tightened the chin strap before she slipped out the door. She arrived at the creek in time to hear Dan splashing across the ford with the horses. Meeting him behind a stand of willows that screened them from the main part of town, she scolded, "What are you doing walking in the water?"

He looked down and wiggled the toes of his boots. "My feet were hot and the water feels real good." Then he sent her a hard look. "You going to be cranky all the way, or is this just a temporary thing?"

"And if I say it's permanent?"

"You can ride alone. You don't need me. In this mood you'd terrify all the Shoshone warriors and Phil Hardesty lumped together."

"That bad, huh?"

"Worse!" He broke into a wide grin.

"Let me help you on your horse," Carrie said, more than willing to drop the subject of her disposition.

"Stand my crutch up so we can find it tonight when we get back."

She leaned it out of sight in the split of a large cottonwood trunk and then came to stand next to him.

"Let me put my arm around your shoulder." He grasped

the saddle horn with his left hand and put his right arm around Carrie's shoulder. Trying not to lean his full weight on her, he lifted his left foot into the stirrup.

"Now, give me a shove," Dan instructed.

Carrie helped lift his weight until he stood in the stirrup. But that wasn't the worst part. She knew the real pain would come when he swung his injured leg over the saddle. Lying flat on the sorrel's neck, Dan slowly raised his right leg and gasped.

Carrie watched the pain twist his mouth and etch lines in his face.

"Please don't do this to yourself," she begged. "I can go alone."

"I'm aware that you can *go* alone," he said when he could breathe again. "It's the *coming back* you seem to have problems with."

Gently he lowered his right leg and set his foot in the stirrup. He straightened up and put his full weight into the saddle.

Anxiously she asked, "How is it?"

"Just an ache. I'll be all right."

Filling a canteen with water, Carrie tied it to the saddle and mounted the horse Dan had chosen for her.

The ride to the agency took just under an hour but the unrelieved heat made it seem longer. Dan rode in his short-sleeved shirt, his light jacket tied to the cantle. Carrie followed his eyes as they remained fixed on the sun-drenched grasslands rising to the foothills. If Phil had come this way, there was no sign of him.

Over the rise now, they rode down toward the modest house, glistening white in the early afternoon sun. There wasn't a buggy or horse in sight. A massive cottonwood cast a wide pool of black shadow over the front yard of the agency. They rode under it and reined up. Against the sunny side of the house a neat bed of brightly colored flowers bloomed and the white lace curtains at the windows rippled slightly in the hot eastern breeze.

"You sure somebody's here?" Dan asked.

"I'm sure. No woman would leave with the windows still open. Not unless she was dragged away by force."

Carrie slid to the ground and looped the reins around the tie rail. "Help yourself to the canteen. I won't be long."

He answered by unfastening the strap over his holstered pistol and checking to be sure it would slide out easily.

Somehow startled by the implications of his action, Carrie nodded briefly, then knocked on the door and waited. As before, she had to knock a second time. The door finally opened a crack. Matwanda stood in the shadows.

"I've come to see Alice," Carrie said, her voice firm.

"Like I told you yesterday, she ain't here."

"Well, I've ridden all the way out here for the cape she borrowed."

"Don't know nothin' 'bout no cape," Matwanda muttered sourly.

Seeing the door about to close on her, in desperation Carrie gave it a hard shove. Unexpectedly, the doorknob caught Matwanda in the stomach and she gasped.

Dismayed by the results of her action, Carrie nevertheless stepped quickly inside. She had to know what had happened to Alice! The house was uncomfortably hot and flies droned over everything. Before Matwanda could recover, Carrie hurried down the hall and into Alice's bedroom.

The room was small and comfortably furnished with a single brass bed and a small chair. An oil lamp, cleaned and filled, waited on the oak night stand. Opening the

105

matching wardrobe, Carrie took a quick inventory of Alice's clothes. Nothing seemed to be missing.

Carrie found the cape she had loaned Alice hanging on a coat rack in the corner and took it. Checking the dressing table, Carrie found all Alice's toilette articles intact. Even her toothbrush was in its holder. Pulling up the bedspread, Carrie looked under the bed. Alice's matching satchels were neatly stored and not one was missing.

Footsteps thumping down the hall toward the bedroom interrupted Carrie's searching. She hastily straightened the dust ruffle, opened the door, and stepped out of the room. She met Matwanda just outside.

"I'm sorry Alice hasn't returned," Carrie said. "Any idea when she might be back?"

"She packed for at least a fortnight. Near took a mule to carry all her things." The woman crowded Carrie toward the door. "I'd save myself a trip if'n I were you. I'll tell Mrs. Skyler you called and she can come to town when she's back."

Carrie had retreated down the hallway until she felt the knob of the front door in the middle of her back. She fumbled for it and let herself out. Without a backward glance, she ran to her waiting horse and Dan.

She tied the cape on the saddle, then, taking the reins, she mounted. She and Dan turned the horses back over the road they had just traveled.

"No Alice, I take it," Dan said, breaking the silence as they rode away from the house.

"Oh Dan, I'm so worried about her! That awful woman told so many lies. She said Alice had packed for a fortnight, but there isn't a thing missing in her room."

"You're sure about that?"

"Yes, I am. Alice lived across the hall from me for nearly

a year. I know her clothes. Nearly everything she owned was in her room, including her matched set of luggage. She didn't even take her toothbrush."

Carrie swallowed the threatening sobs. "Dan, I'm so frightened for her. I'm sure she's been kidnapped—or something even worse!"

"Any idea why?"

"Maybe she heard something she wasn't supposed to know. And where has Jed *really* gone? It's *not* to quiet the Indians."

Dan glanced at the sun. "There's still plenty of daylight left. Let's do a bit of exploring. Are you game?"

"You're asking the lady who rode into the Indians' sacred mountains a question like *that*?"

Dan laughed. "Let's go."

He took off his soft, worn hat, bleached by summers of hot sun, and raked through the sweat-damp strands of chestnut-brown hair. In the full, unshaded light, his sun-darkened face was determined. He reset his hat and turned to her, a question in his eyes.

Carrie nodded in silent, unspoken agreement.

Together they turned their horses west into the timbered foothills, picking up the game trail Carrie had followed earlier. Riding onto the reservation, they traveled toward the Owl Mountains.

Chapter 10

Carrie and Dan rode north in the late afternoon heat. The fragrance of the pines filled the forest air and the soft humus of their needles deadened the horses' hoofbeats.

As Dan and Carrie followed the game trail that twisted up the ridge, Carrie could still spot traces of Phil's previous presence there. But once again, at the talus slope near the top of the ridge where Carrie had spent the night in the cave with Piube, she lost his tracks.

They stopped to let their horses blow after the climb, and Dan threw back his head to scan the impenetrable granite wall before them.

"You're sure Hardesty came this way?"

Fire surged through her at the inference in his tone. "I'm sure!" she said, clenching her jaw and swallowing the other comments she had the urge to make. It took no big talent to follow a set of prints on a trail. Men!

Urging her horse ahead of Dan's on the trail, she spotted a thin split in the face of the mountain but there seemed no way to get into it. Rocks, trees, and dense underbrush blocked the way. Yet, she knew Phil had to have gone in there. If he had ridden off in any other direction, she would have seen him or his tracks.

Quickly swinging to the ground, she knelt. He *had* to have left marks, a sign, something she missed before in the shadows of evening. She crawled along, examining each rock.

"What do you think you're doing down there like that?" asked Dan in disbelief.

"You mean you've never done this to pick up a trail?" she shot over her shoulder.

"Of course I have. Anyone who knows what they're doing has. But what are *you* doing?"

Carrie's fingers closed around a good-sized rock. This was too much! She purposely exhaled a bit of the fire before she leaped to her feet and turned on him.

"And, Mr. Dan King, just what makes you think I don't know what I'm doing?"

Dan seemed startled by her reaction and more than a little uncomfortable. "Well . . . er . . . ah," he stammered, "Tracking's not a skill normally attributed to a woman."

She planted her small fists firmly on her hip bones and glared into his confused face.

"Which means it's a skill totally reserved for the keen eyes of the superior male? Is that what you think?"

"Hadn't given the matter *any* thought. Never came up before." He was baffled by her anger and his voice reflected it. Dropping his eyes to her hand, he asked, "You planning to use that rock for anything specific?"

She turned her fist over and beheld the irregular piece of granite. In her anger, Carrie had forgotten she had it in her hand. However, she had no intention of letting Dan know that.

"I'm still trying to decide," she answered, her voice still showing her exasperation. Keeping an accusing eye on Dan, she casually tossed the rock in the air and caught it several times. She pursed her lips and paused between each toss as though weighing what to do with the object.

Actually, she felt more than a little foolish at her over-reaction. Dan didn't know about her earlier training by Running Bear and, he was right. It wasn't usual for a lady to know the art of tracking. But how could she retreat from her aggressive position and still save face?

She looked at the rock resting in her hand and unconsciously pivoted it with her fingers as she studied her dilemma.

Suddenly, she stopped. Just under her thumb there was a small white scar on the rock. Actually, she knew it could mean little since only yesterday she had ridden a shod pony both up and down this trail. It most likely was made then, but it did offer an excuse to smooth over the growing hostility between Dan and her. She lifted her palm to him.

"What do you make of that?" she asked, pointing to the rock.

His eyes narrowed and the muscles in his jaw twitched. "You testing me?"

She gulped. His bewilderment had turned to anger. She hadn't meant to trample quite so hard on his insufferable male ego. Now she had to find a way to neutral ground again. They needed each other if he was to find his cattle and she was to learn Alice's fate.

"No, I'm not testing you. You've spent a great deal more time tracking than I. If you could get off and on a horse with any ease, you'd be down here instead of me. I'm only trying to be your eyes." She continued to extend her hand with the rock.

The wait seemed interminable before he reached out and lifted it from her palm. He turned it into the light, examining it closely. "Where'd you pick it up from?"

She pointed the toe of her boot at the general area. "See if you can find any more that are marked."

She walked slowly along and, as she studied the trail more closely, she realized both sets of prints left by her horse were still visible. But she had ridden close to the hill and away from the edge of the canyon below. The marked rock had been on the canyon side.

Ahead, the trail turned around a large boulder which had broken off the cliff above. Currant bushes grew in thick clumps around it, blocking any normal attempt to ride by. She stopped and peered closely around the base, then continued a few steps beyond. The marked rocks ceased.

She turned to look at Dan. He had pulled his hat low over his eyes and slouched, arms crossed over the saddle horn, watching her every move.

"Find something?" he asked.

"I don't know," she answered honestly. Backtracking to the last sign, she stooped to examine each rock and the dirt in between. There it was! Only a partial print, but one of the worn shoe. She took the measure of the horse's stride and, straddling the trail so as not to destroy anything, she inched her way along. Again, just before she came to the rock, all signs stopped. Simply vanished, leaving no trace of Phil's horse.

She looked through the prickly thicket. "You don't suppose Phil rode into that, do you?"

"Is this where the tracks end?"

"Right here."

"Look for signs of broken branches," Dan instructed.

Carrie knew what to do, but since he was beginning to warm slightly she thought she'd better keep her tongue civil. She fingered the branches she could reach but she didn't relish diving into the midst of the inhospitable berry bushes.

As though reading her mind, he said, "You're going to have to go *in* them to tell where he went."

She hesitated. She wasn't going to wade into the midst of those brambles and get scratched up just to learn Phil hadn't taken that route.

"If you back in they're not so bad," he suggested.

"I'd prefer not going in at all." Slowly, she walked to the upper side of the rock and gingerly parted the bushes, taking care to keep them from her face. It looked less dense here. Hugging the rock, she inched through a small space between it and the rocks.

Once beyond the bushes, she found another game trail winding into the canyon and immediately picked up Phil's tracks. She hurried back to where Dan waited.

"The trail picks up on the other side of the rock," she said as she mounted. "I remember now he made a point of putting on leather chaps. I thought it strange he would wear the extra weight in the August heat . . . but then, Phil does all manner of strange things and it slipped my mind."

"Good work, Carrie," Dan said, the sincerity of his praise ringing in his voice. "Why don't you let me lead your pony through and you meet us on the other side? Save you some scratches."

She wanted to tell him she could ride through those clawing things as well as he could, but she decided that was carrying her independence to the extreme. She had proven enough for awhile. She did as he suggested.

After riding through the canyon which widened into a lush basin, they stopped to rest the horses and drink from a stream so new from its snow birth there had been no time for the sun to take even an edge of the chill off. Scooping up handsful of water, she rinsed her face and then drank deeply. "Aren't you getting off?" she asked Dan.

"I think I'd better not. Might not make it back up." He looked around at the tree-framed meadow. "This is a beautiful place but there's an odd feeling about it. I wouldn't want to spend the night here."

Carrie handed him the canteen. "So you feel it, too? I wonder if this is the meadow where the two chiefs met in mortal combat?"

Dan drank and wiped his mouth before he answered. "I couldn't say, but I do know that if it is, we're in trouble."

"Why?" Carrie took the canteen and filled it.

"Legend has it that anyone who comes into the forbidden country dies in some violent way."

In the process of tying the canteen to her saddle, she looked over at him. "Dan King, that is the silliest statement I have ever heard. Everyone dies sooner or later. And here in the west, not too many die of old age."

He grinned. "Just you remember my words when you're facing a hanging or scalping. Any woman as independent as you is sure not likely to die in bed."

Carrie laughed heartily at his nonsense. "I've trusted my life to the Lord since I could understand His was the way. I've been well-cared for and I have no doubt that He will continue to do so." Carrie stepped into her saddle and looked at Dan for direction.

His face sobered and his eyes misted over. "You're a

Christian, too," he said softly. "I gave my life to Christ as a child. I could never have survived the tests that have been asked of me without His loving support and care."

Carrie's heart leaped at his words. He *was* a Christian. Suddenly carefree she had to force herself to concentrate on his next words.

"I don't see any tracks around here." His voice had lightened. "Is that a good sign?"

Her delight at his declaration of faith sparkled in her voice, though she made no direct mention of it. It would never do to let him know how much it meant to her.

"If you're asking me if no sign is a good sign, I haven't the slightest notion. Somewhere, though, I remember being told it takes tracks to lead to something." She paused. "Or someone in this case." Her last words killed any levity, for the search for Alice was not a laughing matter and concern filled her again.

Crossing the meadow, they were soon climbing steep, tree-covered hills. So steep, they found it necessary to rest the horses frequently.

"Dan, where would you hide someone if you wanted them out of the way for a few days?" Carrie asked at last as they rested for a moment.

"It would have to be a place that was safe from wild animals at night without keeping a fire."

"Like one of the caves here in these mountains?" Carrie asked.

"I don't know. I'm beginning to think they didn't bring her into the mountains. We've seen no sign of any but Phil's horse," Dan said.

"True, and after all, assuming someone kidnapped her, they probably only want to keep her hidden for a little while. This is a lot of effort for that."

A dark scowl crossed his face. "I hope for her sake

you're right. We're dealing with dangerous men," Dan said, "men who seem capable of anything, including murder, if someone stands in their way."

Dan paused and a thoughtful look stole into his eyes.

"Hardesty's voice keeps haunting me. I've heard it someplace before but I can't put a finger on where. Get the feeling it wasn't under happy circumstances, though."

Carrie felt completely frustrated. "Nothing's making any sense," she said.

Suddenly, Dan exclaimed, "You know, there's an abandoned mine with some pretty good buildings not too far from my ranch," he said. "That's far enough north that, even if Alice escaped, she'd have a long, long walk. Take her several days to make it back to Parke's Crossing and warn anyone."

Dan pulled a rough map out of his shirt pocket. "My ranch is here," he said, pointing to a general area of the map, "the mine is here. And Parke's Crossing would be here."

Carrie leaned over and looked at the map. "You think something is going to happen soon?"

"I do. If they're hiding something—like cattle, maybe—they can't hold them in the same place forever. The grass'll wear out. They're going to have to move them sooner...." Dan stopped in mid-sentence and motioned her to silence.

He started to get off his horse, but she leaped to the ground first.

"What is it?" she whispered.

"We've been riding just below the ridge crest. I thought I heard something on the other side."

Carrie handed him the reins of her pony and climbed the remaining distance to the crest. Through the trees,

115

she could tell there was a valley below, but she couldn't see into it. Hurrying back, she took her field glasses from the saddlebag.

Peering anxiously at her, Dan asked, "See anything?"

"It's so far away and there are so many trees, I couldn't see a thing. Maybe if we ride higher on the ridge we can find a place we can see through or find a trail down."

She mounted again and followed Dan, letting him pick the way through the trees and brushy undergrowth.

He drew to a halt and pointed. Ahead was a clearing where a fire had swept over the land. A new forest was growing, but it wasn't tall enough yet to block the view. They rode to the edge and looked into a box canyon filled with cattle.

"Well, I'll be switched!" Reaching out for Carrie's field glasses, Dan studied the herd intently. "I can find at least a dozen of mine right off and some belonging to my neighbors."

He handed the glasses back to her. "Recognize any of those herders?"

Carrie trained the glasses on each one and studied his features. "I've seen all of them at one time or another this summer, but never together and only for a meal now and then. They spent most of their time at Phil's saloon and then about sundown, they'd ride out."

"I saw one of the drifters that came in yesterday and sent Phil off in such a lather," Dan added, crooking his good leg around the saddle horn. He sat for several minutes, quietly thinking. "I can't figure what they're holding the cattle here for. And where's Jed? Doesn't he know about this much beef being stored on the reservation?" He turned troubled eyes to Carrie. "None of it makes any sense."

"I still think if we could find Alice, we'd have the

beginnings to unravel this."

Dan looked at the sun. "Well, we aren't going to solve anything today. We'll be lucky to make it back to town by dark even if we start now."

"Any chance of finding how they brought the cattle in? It certainly wasn't the way we've come."

"We can't try now. They could easily spot us."

"Then, let's wait for dark. It seems a shame to have come this close and miss the chance," Carrie urged.

"You don't give up easily, do you?"

"If I did, Phil would have bought me out and driven me off years ago."

Dismounting, Carrie took a large knife from her saddlebag, removed its scabbard, and cut some fresh pine boughs. Piling them in overlapping rows, she soon had a springy bed. When she was satisfied with her work, she helped Dan from his horse. Careful as she was, though, he groaned several times before she got him stretched out on the makeshift bed. Taking a handkerchief, she dampened it from the canteen and wiped the perspiration from his pain-twisted face.

"I think you've overdone royally," she scolded as she unpinned his pants leg and examined the bandage. It was clean, so Dan's wound hadn't opened. She silently thanked the Lord for that much.

"A nap and a bit of food will fix me up fine," he said in an obvious attempt to minimize his weakness.

Carrie's jaw dropped. "I only brought water. All I have in the way of solid nourishment is a few dried elk strips I grabbed from the pantry."

"I'm in no position to be picky. That's more than I have."

She fished out the meat dried to stick-like consistency and handed him half. They ate without further conversation, but Carrie would have given much to know what was going on in Dan's head. She guessed it had something to do with her because when he thought she wasn't looking he'd shoot a quick glance at her.

Carrie rested against a pine tree and Dan, exhausted beyond the effects of the pain, closed his eyes at last in a sound sleep. Carrie thought she'd just rest her eyes against the bright sun, but when she opened them again, the sun had set and the air was taking on its customary night chill. She shivered and watched the horizon as the first star of evening brightened. The little rhyme of childhood came from nowhere, "I wish I may, I wish I might, have the wish I wish tonight." She looked at Dan and his eyes opened, less dark and brooding than before, and fastened on hers.

Chapter 11

Dan felt the old restlessness begin to stir as he watched Carrie. In the quiet night he drifted into the fantasy, glowing and warm, that had become a part of his loneliness. In the two years since Anna's death, he had lived with her in his imagination.

He often followed her through a day's routine duties, remembering with painstaking detail how the skin of her firm arms shone as she kneaded the bread dough; how her long shapely fingers fluttered the flowers from her garden into colorful arrangements that brightened each room. Thought how she greeted him with such joy at the end of each day and seemed to fairly burst with gladness when he had been away longer and returned.

When they had learned she was in a family way, how close they had become! Then, he could hardly bear to leave her for even the day. He hadn't left her at all when it came close to her time.

In his pain-filled memory, he relived the race for the midwife. Though he had ridden like the wind, when they returned the baby had come and he found his tiny son and his beautiful wife dead.

The haunting regrets tortured his waking moments. If they had lived in a city, she would have had help. Anna and his son would be alive today. His forehead knotted into a deep scowl with these thoughts and again he vowed never to take a woman to wife while he lived in a such a wilderness.

"It's a lovely night," Carrie said, breaking into his reverie. Her soft, husky voice disturbed him, tempting him to forget some of the vividness of Anna and his promise.

Dan clenched his jaws. "Best part of summer," he returned, making his voice flat and unreadable. "Guess we'd better go," he added.

Wearily, he eased to his feet and let Carrie help him onto his horse. He let his legs dangle free of the stirrups, resting the injured one as they rode the ridge above the canyon.

At last, they spotted the glow of a large campfire reflecting off the back wall of the box canyon. Laughter and talk floated lightly on the night air. Dan reined up, folded his arms, and leaned on the saddlehorn. "This far into sacred ground, they apparently feel safe from both Indians and whites."

"Certainly aren't making any effort to hide their presence," Carrie agreed, her voice a soft whisper.

"With so many men around the fire, I doubt they're keeping a night watch," Dan observed.

"Let's hope not. Make it a lot easier for us if they don't know we're here," Carrie replied.

Setting his feet in the stirrups, Dan rode cautiously down the steep trail into the canyon. The bright moonlight lit the way. Carrie followed a discreet distance behind, her pony making scarcely a sound.

Occasionally Dan glanced back at her. Conflicting thoughts crossing his face were hidden by the darkness. *Carrie's some different woman,* Dan thought. *Tracks like an Indian, works like a slave, and rides like a man. Yet she stays every inch a lady while doing it. She can even handle Hardesty without losing her dignity. And most unusual of all, she's a Christian. Not many of them here on the frontier.*

"There's a trail big enough to match the Chisholm coming up alongside the stream," Carrie commented as they reached the canyon floor.

Roused from his thoughts, Dan slowly focused his eyes and his attention on the wide, hoof-trodden path. Forcing himself to concentrate, he said, "They've been moving a lot of cattle."

"Hmmm," was all she said.

Glancing at Carrie, Dan found that she had swung far out of her saddle and was riding nearly upside down as she studied the tracks with the eye of an expert. He hated to admit it, even to himself, but she was probably better at tracking than he.

"See anything interesting?"

"I don't know if you'll find this interesting, but they've been moving herds both in and out and almost on top of each other."

She returned to a normal riding position and loosened the chin tie on her hat, letting it fall to rest on her back.

Dan couldn't take his eyes off her hair. In the moonlight, the thick strands shone like silver and he wondered what she would look like with the disciplined wings let loose to flow. He pictured her removing the combs and pins, pulling all the hair to one side over her shoulder, and brushing out the knot in back. Although he silently chastised himself for his infidelity to Anna's memory, he seemed incapable of dislodging Carrie from his mind.

At last Dan muttered, "Where are they taking the cattle and why?" He forced his thoughts to the puzzle facing them. One thing was sure. Phil Hardesty was the hub around which everything turned. The answers lay there.

They rode unchallenged along the trail through the narrow, deep-cut canyon. As they broke out of the gorge, they found a crude brush fence hiding the entrance. It was easily moved by a rider on horseback and replaced without leaving a sign. However, there was no trail on this side and heavy trees blotted out most of the moonlight.

"Must have driven the herds in the creek to wash away tracks," Carrie said. "A good Indian trick."

Unable to contain his curiosity any longer, Dan finally asked, "How did you learn so much about tracking?"

As they rode companionably in the still night, Carrie told him the story of Running Bear.

"That explains it," Dan exclaimed. "Much as I hate to admit it, with a teacher like that, you're probably the best around."

Startled by the admission, and inordinately pleased by it, Carrie simply stared at him and didn't deny it.

Suddenly, with no warning, they broke from the dense forest onto the flatland. Now they rode like gray ghosts in the moon-bathed night. Dan kept his eyes from Carrie, not trusting his thoughts. But it did little good. The silence between them was alive, crackling with awareness of each other. Valiantly Dan tried to summon a picture of Anna and found Carrie's face sliding in and out of focus instead. It angered him that he could not control his thoughts better. If his leg didn't ache so desperately, he told himself, he'd set heels to his horse and ride away from this woman, away from her enchantment over him.

His leg was the excuse Dan gave, but deep inside he knew he wouldn't ride from Carrie. Couldn't. His breath caught as the thought became real. He hadn't broken his vow not to bring another woman to this country. Carrie was a *part* of Wyoming. She understood how it was and *chose to live here.*

The spark of feeling after two years of the numbness of death made him lightheaded. He wanted to reach out and touch Carrie, hold her hand, feel its warm weight in his. He thought about last night as they'd sat together on the hotel steps and remembered how her hand was built— delicate bones but the fingers were short and square. They were hands that could wash and cook and heal. Deceptively gentle hands filled with the strength to survive this hostile country.

He started to speak, then thought better of it. He forced himself to picture Anna on her death bed instead. *For all her love of Wyoming, Carrie would be no different. Without help in a birthing, she'd die, too. No, Dan, my friend, stop dreaming and keep a hold on reality. When the time comes, you'll have to make the choice—a wife or the ranch. Can't have it both ways.*

The yearning in him subsided. The decision relieved his mind. Inside his heart turned hard again and the spark died. The familiar cold returned and he rode in a brooding silence. Carrie glanced at him uncertainly several times but made no attempt at conversation. It was sometime after midnight when they reached Parke's Crossing again. They let their horses drink from the stream before moving into the deep shadows of the cottonwood grove.

Carrie slipped to the ground and tied her paint, finally breaking the long silence. "Town seems unusually lively for this time of night, don't you think?" she whispered as she brought him his crutch.

Dan kicked his feet free and let his legs dangle for a minute. A wave of weariness nearly caused him to drop out of the saddle. He couldn't remember the last time he'd felt so tired. If only that leg would stop pounding! Taking a deep breath against the inevitable agony, he eased to the ground. Carrie steadied him until he caught his balance.

"You go on up," she urged. "I'll take care of the horses, then come have a look at your leg."

Dan nodded. He needed no further urging. He could almost feel the mattress under his back as he started for the wash house. Behind him, he could hear Carrie uncinching the saddles, preparing to rub down the tired animals before she took them to the livery.

Even in his weariness, though, Dan had felt a strange uneasiness as they rode into town. Now he cautiously kept in the shadows and took great care to be quiet. A horse nickered softly, but the sound didn't come from the livery stable. He prayed their horses in the grove wouldn't answer. Another did answer, but the sound seemed to come from in front of the hotel.

Still in the shadow of the trees, Dan paused. On the veranda of Phil's store, silhouetted in front of the lighted window stood a soldier, his rifle slung over his shoulder as though on guard duty. The soldier looked in both directions along the street, stepped off the veranda and crossed toward the back of the hotel. Two more men came from behind the livery and one came from the front of the hotel.

Dan breathed a sigh of relief as he realized the soldiers he had sent for to help find Carrie had arrived at last. About to step out of the shadows and onto the trail to the wash house, he hesitated briefly.

"Any luck?" one asked.

"Can't find a trace of the slippery skunk," someone answered.

Dan halted in mid-step. Who were they talking about? It obviously wasn't Carrie.

"He hasn't been near the wash house. I've been on guard there since just after dark," said another.

"His horse still isn't back in the stable. We just checked again on the off chance he sneaked it past us."

It was him—Dan—the Army wanted! But why? He couldn't think of a thing he had done in his entire life to bring about the kind of venom in the voices of these men.

"I want to be the one who slaps the horse from under him when they hang the mangy mongrel." One voice added. "Anybody sells whiskey to the Indians deserves the worst to my way of thinking."

Dan didn't wait to hear more. He had to catch Carrie before it was too late. He swung around and hobbled to the grove where she was just finishing with the horses.

"I've got to leave," he whispered. "Help me up."

"Wha . . . "

Dan put his hand over her mouth to silence her. "The Army's after me. Here, stand so you can boost me up."

"Dan," she whispered, "have you lost your mind?" Her eyes widened with fear as she looked into his.

Dan ignored her comments and tightened the cinch on his saddle. "Carrie, help me!" he implored. "They think I'm the one selling whiskey to the Indians."

"That's crazy!"

"I couldn't agree more, but the mood of the soldiers I just overheard isn't one that would allow me to explain. They're talking hanging!" He dropped the stirrup. "Now, help me on my horse. Please!"

Frustration at being unable to mount the horse unaided edged his voice. If he didn't ride out immediately he felt sure he'd be swinging from a rope by noon.

The murmer of the soldiers' voices carried on the still night air though their words were indistinct. Carrie looked in their direction and she hesitated.

"Dan, this is insanity. Your leg isn't up to more riding today. I can hide you someplace." Her eyes pleaded with him.

Dan's hands tightened on the reins as the voices seemed to grow closer. He forced himself to speak calmly. "Where? Once they know you're back they'll turn this town upside down looking for me. And how do you plan to hide my horse?" he asked.

Her face pale with the strain, Carrie stared at him. "I can't bear to think of you riding out again when you're already exhausted. It could kill you!"

"Standing here is going to get me killed!"

The seconds ticked off with deliberate slowness.

Finally, without words, Carrie moved into position next to the horse and took Dan's crutch. As he swung his leg over into the stirrup, pain seared through him. The agony nauseated him.

Suddenly Dan stiffened.

" . . . check that bunch of trees. Black enough in there to hide half a regiment."

Bending low, he eased his sorrel through the trees and into the stream toward the mountains.

He felt Carrie watching him, a dark blot in darker shadows. For the second time in their short acquaintance, she held his life in her hands.

126

Chapter 12

Untying her horse, Carrie stepped out of the darkness and walked slowly in the direction of the voices.

"Good evening, gentlemen," she said, hoping they couldn't see how stiff her smile was. "I trust I'm not the cause of your being here."

A young man who barely appeared to be of shaving age moved toward her from the group. Carrie noticed that he wore sergeant's stripes.

"Evening to you, ma'am. You Carrie Benson?" he asked, his adam's apple bobbing vigorously in his scrawny neck.

"Yes, I am." Without slowing her steps she walked in the direction of the livery stable, talking as she did so. She hoped he would turn and follow her.

"Out kinda late, aren't you?" he asked, falling into step beside her.

Thank you, Lord, he's coming with me. She smiled up at the soldier. "I went for a ride earlier and kind of got myself lost. Saw a lot of country I hadn't seen before and it took me awhile to find my way back."

Carrie sauntered down the street toward the stable with the knot of soldiers in her wake.

"Take your horse?" one of them offered.

"That would be most thoughtful of you." She handed him the reins but kept on walking. "You weren't looking for me, then? Why are you on duty? Will you be here all night?" she asked.

"I sure hope not, ma'am. If that money-hungry scoundrel, Dan King, rides in soon, we can lock him up and get some sleep."

"Dan King? Is that why you're here? To capture him?"

"That's right. Got a reliable tip he's the one been selling whiskey to the Indians. Man willing to jeopardize innocent people's lives for the sake of money—well, he don't deserve to live, way I look at it."

They reached the livery and one of the soldiers opened the wide door. Rusty hinges squealed at the disturbance. The inside was thick with blackness but Carrie knew the building well so she moved confidently down the aisle.

A loud clatter and a few muffled exclamations told her one or more of the men following her had run into trouble.

"Watch your language," the young sergeant snapped. "Light a match and find a lantern."

"There's a lantern hanging on a nail right next to the door on the left-hand side," Carrie offered.

There was enough light from the open door that she could see to continue on through the building to the corral in back. Once there, she unfastened the hackamore and a soldier hurried over to lift off the saddle.

The lantern flared to life as they returned inside. The other soldiers were walking slowly, examining the horses wakened by the disturbance. They hung their heads over the stall barriers and silently watched the proceedings.

"Any look like King's horse?" the tall leader asked.

"Ain't a sorrel in the lot, much less a top animal like was described to us."

"Thank you all so much for the help," Carrie said, hoping to distract them. "If you'll come with me to the hotel, I could fix you some coffee and pie."

The men looked at each other and then to the sergeant. He took his position at her elbow. "Looks like it's going to be a long night," he said and a gentle pressure on her arm urged her out of the stable. "That offer is much appreciated."

"Are there just six of you?" she asked.

"Afraid so. We're all that could be spared right now." They walked in a slow parade across the dusty street. "Why'd you want to know that, ma'am?" he asked, suddenly sounding suspicious as they mounted the steps to the hotel lobby. His voice seemed a touch less warm and Carrie could have sworn his grip tightened on her arm.

She smiled at him. "So I would know how many to fix for. If there were others, I was going to suggest they be invited in, too."

He blushed and the adam's apple jerked spasmodically, revealing the extent of his discomfort. "Sorry. I've grown overly suspicious of people and their intentions while being out here in Wyoming."

"Don't think a thing about it," Carrie said easily as she led the troops into the dining room. "You gentlemen sit down and I'll have refreshments out to you in a few

129

minutes." She propped the door open between the kitchen and dining room, and the sergeant seated himself so he could see her.

Apparently Elsa had only recently retired, for the stove was still hot and the fire banked. A large pot of still warm coffee sat on the back and pies covered with cheesecloth lined a shelf in the buttery. *Bless you, Elsa.*

Carrie quickly filled coffee cups and set large pieces of apple pie before the men. When everyone was served, she pulled up a chair and sat down to visit. Though she was so tired she could scarcely focus on the conversation, it seemed an excellent opportunity to keep the men's attention away from their search for Dan. If they grew sleepy enough and she could convince them to go to bed, she could slip back to the grove and erase the tell-tale tracks left by Dan's horse. That would give him such a head start they would have difficulty ever tracking him.

Her heart ached at the thought of Dan riding out into the hills again. She knew he was tired, hungry, and his leg was undoubtedly throbbing its distress in earnest by now. She worried about how he would get on the horse once he got off and, with no crutch, how he would move around when he was off.

" . . . don't you think so?"

Lost in her own thoughts, she hadn't paid attention to what was being said at the table. "Weeell, I don't know," she stalled.

The sergeant looked shocked. "You don't know how you feel about the Indians? You're the first one I've met who doesn't have definite opinions about what should be done to or with 'em."

Trying to extricate herself from the hole her inattention had dropped her into, she asked, "How do most that you've met feel?"

"They're afraid of the Indians, many with very good reason, and they dislike them for past and present injuries. They want them kept prisoners on the reservation and killed if they leave."

"Well, *I* certainly don't feel that way," she announced emphatically. All the soldiers turned to look at her. With them hanging on her words, she told of her experiences with Running Bear and Washakie. She drew the tales out until her audience could hardly stay awake.

The clock chimed the hour of two and she yawned. "I doubt that Mr. King is going to return to Parke's Crossing at this hour. May I offer you gentlemen beds? If you don't rest, you'll all be asleep on your feet in the morning if he does come in."

Looking at his exhausted men, the weary sergeant nodded. "We have had a long day. Probably would be best to take a break."

The other five men cast grateful eyes at Carrie as she pushed back from the table and led the way upstairs.

The rooster crowed outside the wash house window and penetrated Carrie's sleep-filled brain. She rolled over on the mattress Dan had been using and stretched.

She had chosen to sleep in the wash house so that she could slip undetected into the woods at the first light. So ignoring her body's plea for more rest, she scrambled to her feet.

She lit the fire in the jack stove, set water to heat, then hurried to the place in the trees where she had cared for the horses. Cutting a willow switch, she brushed away all signs of Dan's horse while making sure the tracks of her paint remained well-defined. Thank goodness they had chosen to ride in the stream for much of the distance away from town.

By the time the soldiers came down for breakfast, Carrie had washed her first load of linens. She was hanging the load of sheets when a couple of the soldiers strolled into the trees. Watching them carefully, she knew at once they knew little about tracking. Dan had nothing to fear if this was the best the Army could send.

Dan, her most pressing concern, was safe. Now, she could turn her full attention to the matter of Alice. Dan had suggested an old ghost town to the north. As soon as she could she would get out her maps and look it up. With Dan gone, Carrie was the only one who seemed to care about finding Alice. It looked like she would have to do it alone.

The soldiers spent a fruitless morning and by noon, when they returned to eat with Carrie's regular guests, they were extremely disgruntled at not finding Dan's tracks either out of or into town.

"Who told you gentlemen Dan King was behind the liquor getting to the reservation?" Carrie asked in an offhand manner as she served dinner.

"I did," Phil said, setting his jaw in a manner which defied anyone to doubt his words.

Carrie pretended innocence. "How do you know for sure Mr. King is the guilty person, Phil?"

Phil tapped his knife on the table for emphasis. "When I got back from my little trip, I came up missing two jugs of prime whiskey. Since King had been working for me, I searched the wash house and found them hidden behind some pillows in his bed."

"You mean you searched *my* property without permission?" Carrie stood over him armed with a full pot of hot coffee.

Phil hopped to his feet, knocking over his chair in the

process. "I didn't think you'd mind, knowing how you feel about anyone who gets liquor to the savages. Besides, you was gone. Nobody here to ask."

Then as an afterthought, he added, "Goes to show you how bad we need a sheriff."

"And I suppose you're nominating yourself for the job?" Carrie shot at him.

"Do you see anyone else capable?"

"Yes. Me!"

Phil threw back his head and laughed. "Carrie, you're one fine woman but I don't see you as a sheriff, even with all your independence."

"That's because you can't see beyond your desire to have the security of the law to cover your own tracks!" Carrie bit firmly on her tongue. If she didn't stop, she'd say more than she wanted to and jeopardize Dan. Changing her tone of voice and the direction of the conversation, she asked, "Elsa was here. Did you ask her?"

"She'd only have said 'no.' " Phil backed slowly out of the dining room as they talked.

"And so would I." She left him standing in the middle of the lobby and returned to serving her dinner guests.

"Ma'am," the young sergeant said quietly, "I saw those bottles with my own eyes."

"Of course you did. That's not evidence against Dan King. Phil undoubtedly put them there so you would. Have you thought how Mr. King would have carried them across the street with one hand holding a crutch? That would have meant chancing two trips with no one seeing him. Doesn't seem a terribly smart thing to do."

The dining table grew silent, the only sounds the clink of utensils. Carrie vanished into the kitchen until she heard the chairs scrape, the signal the men were leaving.

"I'm leaving now to see if I can find Alice," Carrie told

133

Elsa. "Her disappearance is being explained as a short trip at Jed's suggestion to get her out of danger in case of an Indian attack. But I don't think Jed's really aware of anything Alice does. He's under some kind of terrible shadow that's threatening to destroy them both."

"I know it won't do any good to warn you not to go," Elsa said, obviously resigned to Carrie's sudden departures, "but please be careful. I think you're in the middle of some big stakes and those in the game are playing for keeps."

"I know. It's taking all my faith in the Lord to keep going. I'd like to send the Army after Alice and forget the whole mess. I almost wish Dan King had ridden into some other town."

"Why *don't* you send the Army after Alice?"

"Because I don't know for sure where she is and whoever is guarding her might see the soldiers, panic, and kill Alice. I can't take that chance. When I find her and get to the bottom of this mess, that will be time enough to get them involved. Besides, they might tell Phil. I'm not sure how yet, but Phil Hardesty is up to his crooked neck in this. I can't risk his knowing."

"Phil may already know where she is if he's as thick with Jed as you think."

Carrie hadn't thought of that. That made things much worse. Alice might already be dead. Phil didn't seem to have any scruples at all, and if Alice got in his way, he'd see she was removed.

Carrie slowly raised her eyes to meet Elsa's. Fear lined her face as she said, "This is getting out of hand, Elsa. I'm really scared."

"So am I, and I don't think you should ride out alone."

"Who do you suggest I ask to go with me?"

"You know perfectly well there isn't anyone since Dan's gone." Elsa turned to the sink, ending the unsatisfactory conversation.

Carrie hesitated, staring for a few moments at Elsa's back. Then she went up to her room to change clothes. She looked from her window in time to see the soldiers riding out of town in the direction of the fort. That clinched it. A hard certainty settled around her heart. Carrie was Alice's only hope.

Chapter 13

The trail dropped with quick turns and sharp angles toward the bottom of the canyon. A flood of unshadowed noon day sun reflected off sheer, wind-polished cliffs, turning the canyon into a well of sweltering heat.

After two days in the saddle, Carrie rode trance-like, exhausted from the intense and unrelieved heat. Though she had traveled up from the gorge and onto wooded slopes, there was no breeze to break the stifling heat.

Hotter than I remember it ever being, she thought as she paused to rest her pony.

The thin mountain air carried shrill and varied bird songs. To break the heat induced stupor, Carrie forced herself to concentrate on them. Farther on the slope grew much steeper and she relaxed her grip on the reins, letting the sturdy little paint set its own pace on the zig-zagging trail.

The distance hadn't looked nearly so great on her sketchy maps. She'd had no idea it would take so long. She should have known that it was a considerable distance when Dan said he lived so far north he didn't know about Parke's Crossing. He had said the ghost town and mine were close to his ranch which meant it was also near Montana Territory. But the whole thing hadn't really registered until now for Carrie had never ventured so far from home before.

Wondering if she was lost, Carrie stopped and unfolded the map she had sketched from memory. No, there were the high snowpacked peaks to her left. The ghost town Dan had shown her on his rough map should be at the foot of them. But going north in this country didn't mean a straight line unless she wanted to climb steep slopes all the time and then come to a cliff with no way down. By the time she found ways around, she sometimes traveled three or four miles to cover one.

Carrie dismounted and walked for awhile, leading the horse as she went. It felt good to stretch her legs, as the steepness leveled out. Then, almost without warning, she found herself on a deeply rutted wagon road. *Probably used to haul the ore,* she thought. *I must be near the mine.* Excitement surged through her and she had a great urge to tiptoe in case there were guards around Alice. She was sure Alice was here. It was a perfect hiding place.

Stopping just inside the last of the trees, Carrie saw that the road formed two deep tracks across an open meadow, a small green spot cupped inside the hills. Carrie let her horse drink from the small stream and graze while she finished the last of the biscuits and dried meat she had brought. As she washed down the final mouthful with cold water from the stream, she tried not to think what she would do for food tomorrow.

137

Refreshed, she skirted the meadow and continued up a path which led into a deep draw lined with thick brush and rocks. Making her way along the rocks, Carrie finally reached the crest, and saw the old town! She turned off the path and into the trees. If there was someone down there, she didn't want to be a clearly silhouetted target.

Carrie stared down onto what she hoped were unoccupied, weathered buildings. A few carried ambitious names such as the Big Strike, the Boston House, the Gilded Cage, and all grasped at the faint memories of delirious nights of celebrating, devastating gambling losses, and costly love and death.

A welcome breeze blew tumbleweeds through the town and carried the creak of doors and the bang of shutters to Carrie. Fixing her field glasses on the scene, she slowly and carefully examined each building. She could see nothing, but that didn't mean anything. Glancing at the sun, she decided to wait until dark before entering the ghost town. She would present a fine enough target going down that bare hill in the moonlight.

Twilight drew the color from the landscape, then night slid in from the east. Night sounds, tenuous at first, gathered courage and filled the air. Carrie regarded this as a good sign. The sky became a panoply of stars and Carrie knew it was time.

Though she tried to be quiet, the darkness hid loose stones and debris that rolled with clinks and thumps down the side of the hill marking her journey. Dark patches of brush offered sanctuary for the night animals, and when a rabbit hopped in front of Carrie, she forced back a scream. Her horse shied and whinnied. An answer came from below.

Her stomach knotted and her heart raced in her throat. The horse sounded close and Carrie flattened behind a rock. She stayed motionless, straining to hear. At length, the night settled down again and Carrie moved forward cautiously. At last she entered the town, carefully staying in the deepest shadows, looking for the horse—and the rider. But she saw nothing—and no one.

Looking up at the high ground ahead of her, Carrie saw the mine itself. Leaving the silent, empty buildings behind, Carrie chose an indirect route through the trees to the top of the closest ridge. Here walking was easy, the ground even and grass-covered. But she could see a higher ridge and knew if she was to proceed quietly, she would have to leave her horse. She tied him to a tree and loosened his saddle. The climb was steep, up rocks and through crevices, where Carrie grabbed roots and branches to pull herself along. A game trail finally led her to the top. Praying she wouldn't make a misstep, she walked stealthily along the crest of this ridge.

Below her she could see the vague, darker outline of the mine works and the crushing mill. In the dark, Carrie eased her way down to the level shelf where the open mine shafts and a small, dilapidated equipment shed stood.

She took a step toward the shed, accidentally kicked a rock, and sent it spinning over the edge. She froze as it rolled and clattered all the way to the bottom. The noise echoed through the canyon and Carrie's horse neighed. The other horse answered, but now the sound came from across the way.

Carrie waited long, fear filled moments, but no one came to investigate. Wiping sweaty palms on her skirt, she wished fervently this was a dream she would wake from in her own bed. She must be totally mad to think she could outsmart Phil, Jed and anyone else involved, and rescue Alice alone.

The shed, tilted slightly where a corner of it had sunk

into a trench washed by spring thaws, stood at the side of the mine entrance. There was a small window without glass, and shutters on unoiled hinges swung gently in the wind to their own squeaking rhythm. The only door hung part way open, sagging and twisted until it no longer fit the frame.

Carrie picked up a stick, the only thing she could find for a weapon, and moved toward the opening. She shoved the door back with her foot. Two bats flew out and a small scream escaped before she could clamp her lips over it. The sides and corners of the room were dark. She stepped inside and was greeted by silence and an oppressive sense of someone waiting in the still darkness. She wished desperately for a light, but knew she was shaking so badly she couldn't have held a lighted candle if she'd had one.

Breaking the bonds of her terror Carrie whispered, "Alice?"

Rustlings, thumpings and gruntings came from the back of the shed.

"Oh, Alice, I hope that's you." Carrie fought down the urge to run toward the sound. She knew these old buildings had rotten floorboards and holes. Though the moon had finally risen, she still took her time as she moved through the shadows toward the sounds.

At last, she stood looking down on an almost unrecognizable Alice. The dim light revealed Alice's bound hands and feet. Choked noises came through a gag over her mouth. Long, untamed ropes of hair fell over her face. Her clothes were dirty and torn.

"Alice!" Carrie exclaimed and hurried to untie her.

Alice fell into Carrie's arms. "Water," she croaked when the gag was removed and she could speak.

"Oh, Alice, I don't have any with me. The canteen's with my horse."

The wind shifted and cool air blew down the canyon. The sudden cold sent uncontrollable shivers through Alice.

"T-there's a blanket in the c-corner," Alice said, with chattering teeth.

Carrie found the dirty thing and laid it over Alice. "I'll hurry down for the water and be right back," she promised.

Alice clutched at Carrie. "No! Please don't leave me."

"Is anyone guarding you?" Carrie asked in a soft voice.

"No. They come with water and food. They untie me, let me walk around a little. Then I eat. I do that twice a day. I'm left alone, tied up the rest of the time. They ride off down the canyon. I can hear them go."

"Then it's safe for me to leave. I won't be long. You and I both need a drink. Is that your horse I keep hearing?"

"Yes. He's in some kind of shed on the other side of the canyon. I don't know if they're taking care of him or not."

"I'll see to him while I'm down there."

The moonlight revealed a well-used path down the side of the mountain. Thankful for the light, Carrie found Alice's horse easily and after getting hers, she watered both animals in the shallow creek trickling through the canyon. When they had drunk their fill, she brought them up the trail and staked them close to the shed, hidden in the trees. Bringing the canteen and her own blanket, Carrie gave Alice a drink and settled down beside her for what was left of the night.

Alice was so relieved to see Carrie, she wouldn't let her rescuer out of her reach. She clutched Carrie through the night and cried out if Carrie moved. This kept Carrie awake and made morning seem a long time coming. At last, however, the sky lightened and blue-white streaks shot up from behind the eastern ridge.

"What time do they usually come to take care of you?" Carrie asked, stretching away some of the stiffness.

"Not real early. I don't know how far away they're camped, but they don't seem to get here until around mid-morning."

"We need to talk now, then. Who's keeping you prisoner here—and why?"

"I don't know the men, but Jed let them take me." Her voice caught and she struggled with the tears that threatened.

"He didn't say a word when they came for me. Made them bring a cape for me, is all, and tried to give me a blanket. They wouldn't let me have that, though."

Carrie was thunderstruck. What on earth had gotten into that man? When they had first come to Parke's Crossing, he had acted like he adored Alice. He'd been so sweet and thoughtful Carrie had found herself slightly envious that a woman would be treated so.

"Why, Alice? Why?" was all she could say.

"I don't know. I was dusting his desk one day last week and picked up a sheaf of papers. He came in just then, grabbed them from my hands, and almost hit me." A sob wrenched its way out from deep in her throat.

"Do you know what was in the papers?"

"No, I didn't try to read them. Truth was, I'd had a bit more to drink than I should have and everything was blurry."

"Does Jed know that?"

"He didn't give me time to say anything. He hustled me to my room and locked me in. Before I knew it, I was tied to a horse and two men were bringing me here."

Alice drew a deep shuddering breath and wiped the tears into smudges on her dirty cheeks.

Carrie's heart turned leaden. She knew that their lives were in jeopardy if anyone found them. And, on top of that, she didn't know where Dan was or how he was. She couldn't believe her life had become so wrinkled in such a short time.

"Alice," Carrie said firmly, "we've got to get out of here. Do you remember which direction your guards seem to ride when they come up here?"

"I've tried to listen, but sound gets so distorted in the canyon, I'm never sure. They may even come from different ways."

Alice looked in helpless woe at Carrie. "Not much help am I?"

"It's not your fault. I couldn't place your horse last night for the very same reason. I think, under the circumstances, we'd be better off riding among the trees for awhile. I'm going to try to find Dan King's ranch. If we can get past those watching you, that should be a safe spot to hide until we get this whole mess straightened out."

The women were soon ready to leave and Carrie cautiously led the way down and out of the canyon. "Are you hungry, Alice?" she finally asked, breaking their self-imposed silence.

"Yes. I'm truly sick of rancid biscuits and moldy beef not properly dried."

Alice turned expectant eyes on Carrie.

"Maybe I shouldn't have brought up the subject," Carrie apologized. "I don't have any more food, but ... look ahead. Do I see berry bushes?"

"Oh, Carrie—huckleberries! My mouth is fairly watering with anticipation!"

They dismounted and picked and ate as fast as they could. Looking at Alice, Carrie laughed. "You should see your face! You look like a two-year-old, purple from ear to ear with hands to match."

"Is the pot calling the kettle black? You don't exactly look well-groomed," Alice retorted. "But don't these taste good! I can't remember when anything has seemed so delicious."

Carrie saw a large bush a few steps farther into the trees and urged Alice to join her.

Alice needed no persuasion and gathered her skirts to leap the fallen log in her path.

"When we have stripped this bush, my hunger will be thoroughly satisfied. How about yo . . . "

Carrie turned to see Alice's eyes widen and her smeared face pale under its purple tint. Following Alice's unblinking stare, she saw four Shoshone sitting silently astride their ponies. Her heart plummeted to her boot tops and left her breathless. The two parties stared at each other for what seemed like years, until a fifth horseman came quietly through the woods and stopped behind the warriors.

"Washakie!" Carrie exclaimed in relief and recognition.

He nodded in greeting. "Why are you so far from home?" he asked her in Shoshone.

She explained to him about Alice.

"You could make money finding lost people," he said with a smile.

Carrie laughed softly as she remembered Piube. A dull thud behind her drew her attention from Washakie. Alice lay in a heap on the ground.

"Alice!" Carrie bent over the unconscious woman.

Washakie's deep chuckle broke the silence. "She doesn't understand our language?"

Carrie shook her head.

"Probably thinks we are here to take scalps. This is wife of agent. Why white men guard this woman at the mine?"

Surprised, Carrie asked, "You know about that?"

Washakie nodded solemnly. "We know. Would have helped her but didn't want white men on our trail. Don't need more trouble just now."

Then Carrie had what she thought was a brilliant idea. "Washakie, would you hide Alice until I can learn why she is being treated so badly?"

"I owe you and her many favors. Rouse her and we will take her to lodge."

Carrie shook Alice but finally resorted to dousing her with water from the canteen. Sputtering, Alice sat up and wiped back her straggly hair.

"Don't worry, Alice." Carrie reassured her. "They aren't angry with you. You have done many good things for these people. They will take you with them and hide you."

Alice struggled to her feet with Carrie's help. "I'm not afraid of them. Honest. I don't know why I fainted. I'd like to go with Washakie and his men but that is the first place Jed will look for me when he learns I'm missing. If Jed or Phil were to find me with them, it could bring about a brutal retaliation. Thank Washakie for his unselfishness, but I must find some other place," Alice said and bestowed a sweet smile on the warriors.

Washakie nodded his agreement with Alice's words when Carrie repeated them in Shoshone. He and his men started to ride away as silently as they had come.

As the women mounted their ponies, Alice looked forlornly at Carrie, "Where am I going to stay? Maybe I should have gone with them."

Carrie had another idea of where she could hide Alice. The problems she faced were getting them both away from here without being detected and then finding Dan's ranch. Carrie unfolded the crude map and studied it again.

"Washakie," she called suddenly and rode quickly to where he had pulled up to wait for her. "If I can get Alice out of here without being seen, I know a place where she'll be safe. Could you and your braves harrass the men guarding her until we're beyond their reach?"

The braves grinned and Washakie nodded. "Make an interesting morning. Which way you go?"

Carrie pointed to the northwest.

"We lead them southeast," Washakie said. "Give me her cape. Make them think we have taken her."

At Carrie's explanation of the plan, Alice slipped wordlessly out of the stained and torn garment and handed it to Washakie. The tears brimming in her eyes told of her gratitude.

Washakie gave a brief nod, then turned away with his warriors.

Sending silent thanks to the Shoshone, Carrie and Alice watched them disappear into the trees.

"Another example of answered prayer," Carrie said quietly. "God moves in such mysterious ways, I never cease to be amazed."

Alice nodded and allowed herself to cry the tears she had been holding back.

Chapter 14

For more miles than Carrie wanted to think about, the rutted road to Dan's ranch followed the course of a tributary of the Bighorn River. The water, clear and sparkling as cut crystal, gurgled and splashed its way downslope over a bed of gray sand and rounded stones.

Carrie never ceased to thrill at the stirring beauty of this land—not only the majestic sight of it, but also the smells. Tangy resin from the tall pines and firs, fresh aromas from grasses and ripening berry bushes; the sounds of the creek and birds, all of these exhilarated her and made her glad she was alive.

Alice, however, slumped low and limp as a rag doll, looked so pale Carrie was afraid she would faint at any minute. If they didn't find Dan's place soon, Alice would be totally unable to sit a horse.

As they topped another of the many grassy hills, Carrie saw well-built and well-kept log buildings in the distance. Knowing the many miles between ranches, and sure of her general direction, exultation leaped in her heart. "I think the ranch I was looking for is just up the road," she said, hoping the information would encourage Alice.

But even this hopeful news elicited only a weak, "hmmm."

Carrie reached over and took the reins of Alice's horse leading it down the slope toward the spread of buildings dominated by an enormous log barn. A pond in front of the main house reflected the blue sky and dabs of cotton-white clouds. The approach of the horses disturbed several geese that fled, honking, through the high grass.

Carrie and Alice rode under the ranch gate, two tall pines hand hewn to support the thick crosspiece overhead. Hanging on one side of the sturdy log was a carved replica of the white queen and on the other end the black king. Heavy forged black-painted chains connected the two outside figures to the small black and white knight in the center.

Carrie stopped, struck by the significance of what she saw. Chess! Dan King was a chess player. After her father had been killed, Carrie hadn't thought to find another in this unschooled country. But the figures on the gate obviously held more significance than that. The white queen—Dan's wife? Somehow, Carrie hadn't thought about his having a wife. And the little knight in the middle must represent their son.

Her heart beat erratically. How little she knew of this man! How much she had assumed. She forced back the tears threatening to cascade down her face. But there was one consolation. Carrie knew now that Dan King was worthy of her love; he was a godly man who cherished his wife and child above all else, an intellectual man from whom she could have learned and with whom she could have conversed on more than the subject of cattle.

Somehow she felt no better for having made the discovery. She also knew now that there could never be anything between them and that hurt. Hurt far more than she had imagined it could.

A groan from Alice jarred Carrie back to reality. Forcing the pain from her voice, she said hollowly, "Hang on, Alice. We're almost there."

The ranch house was an impressive log building facing the pond and the wide sweep of grassland beyond. Small windows on either side of the front door looked out on a veranda that ran the length of the tidy house. As they drew closer, Carrie could see a swing and a pair of chairs made from elk antlers situated on the veranda to take full advantage of the view in the cool of summer and fall evenings.

About fifty yards from the house stood a long, low building Carrie was sure was the bunkhouse. The small cabin nearby must surely be the domain of the second most important person on any working ranch—the cook. Dan obviously was doing very well. No wonder he was taking such great risks to preserve this place.

Carrie reined up at the bottom of the veranda steps. Tying both horses to the hitching rail, she helped the nearly unconscious Alice to the ground.

"Hold on just a few more minutes. We'll have you safely tucked into bed."

Carrie half-carried, half-dragged the larger woman up the four steps to the veranda. Alice started to fold in Carrie's arms.

"Alice! I can't carry you inside. You *must* walk. You *must.*"

Carrie knocked, then tried the carved doorknob,

praying it would be unlocked. It turned soundlessly, and she opened the large pine door, polished to a high sheen. Staggering under Alice's weight, she managed to get inside and shut the door behind them.

They stood in an imposing, decidedly masculine room. Staring down at them from their mounts around the wall were the heads of elk, deer, moose, bear, antelope. A large bookcase on the far wall was filled with rich, leather-covered volumes. An assortment of handmade chairs covered with a variety of skins was grouped around a massive stone fireplace. On a rack over the fireplace hung an old Spencer rifle, and on a low table in front of the fireplace was spread a magnificent ivory chess set, the pieces in the position of a game in progress.

Carrie drank in the details of this room. Even though he was married, she knew she would never find another man his equal. The moments they had had together and the memory of his home must last her a lifetime for she doubted there would be another for her, ever.

A narrow hallway led off this room and Carrie urged Alice toward it. Instinctively Carrie passed the first door, somehow knowing this must be Dan's room. She tried the next door she came to and stepped into a bedroom, simply furnished with an iron bed, spread with a brightly colored wedding ring quilt and white eyelet lace dust ruffle. A golden oak six drawer dresser with a bevel-edged mirror sat against the inside wall. Carrie studiously avoided the mirror. She could imagine what she looked like and she didn't want it verified.

Lowering Alice into a small oak rocker with blue quilted pillows that softened the wooden slats, Carrie took the pitcher from the matching wash bowl and went in search of water. She couldn't bear to tuck an unwashed Alice into the scrupulously clean bed.

At the end of the hall she found a beautifully furnished

kitchen. The pantry between the kitchen and dining room revealed every kind of cooking pot and utensil a woman could want, but where was the woman this had been furnished for? Aside from being antiseptically clean, the kitchen didn't look like it had been used recently.

Carrie found the water bucket, but it was empty and dry. The pump on the back porch had lost its prime and she was forced to hurry to the nearby stream for water.

A fire was laid in the cook stove. She lit it and, while she waited for the water to heat, she rummaged for something to eat. There were plenty of canned items but nothing fresh. She considered that strange. Even in this high country, it was possible to raise a garden but there were only cheesecloth-covered pans of milk and rounds of butter in the spring house.

As soon as the chill was off the water, Carrie hastened back to bathe Alice. In her exhaustion, Alice slept upright in the rocker. She roused only slightly at Carrie's attempts to remove the most immediate dirt. Opening the oak wardrobe, Carrie found a light flannel nightgown with a lace-trimmed yoke embroidered in pastel flowers. Gently slipping this on Alice, Carrie managed to help the limp figure into the turned-down bed.

Alice immediately snuggled down into the featherbed and sighed. Carrie pulled up the sheet and a light blanket and looked enviously at the sleeping woman. Would that she, Carrie, could curl up so easily and sleep away her troubles.

The room was stuffy, so Carrie went to open the single window through which she could glimpse a field of violet wild asters behind the house. She pulled back the crisp white lace curtains to slide up the sash and saw two granite gravestones under a large cottonwood not far from the house.

Quickly gathering up the towels and water, she tiptoed

151

from the room. Setting the things in the kitchen, she hurried out the back door and over to the markers. She dropped to her knees beside the grassy mounds and her fingers traced the words chiseled in the cold rock. "Here lies Anna Elizabeth King, beloved wife and mother. She died an unnecessary death, killed by a country she could not abide." The epitaph on the other stone read, "Daniel Arthur King, Jr. He died aborning." The date was under it.

Dan had lost his wife and son in the childbirth! A large lump formed in her breast and she added the ache of Dan's loss to her own. The West was a cruel country. It seemed to exact its toll from the best. People like Phil Hardesty lived their rotten lives unscathed while the good who asked so little were cut down in death or, like Alice, destroyed while they still lived. And yet, for all its capriciousness and cruelty, Carrie loved the land. She knew she wouldn't be happy anywhere else.

A sharp whinny from the front yard reminded Carrie that she needed to care for the horses. Rising slowly and brushing at unshed tears, she went to stable the ponies in the big barn she had passed earlier. She pulled off the saddles and set them in the well-supplied tack room. Inside a barrel stored there, she found oats and, leading the horses into stalls, gave each tired animal a pail full.

Thinking it was better if the horses remained unobserved for awhile, Carrie tied them to the manger before she forked them some hay from the freshly cut stack of meadow grass in the corner.

She turned to replace the pitchfork in the hay and found herself looking into the barrel of a rifle held by steady hands. Her jaw dropped and she couldn't get a word past the constriction in her throat.

"You always come to place uninvited, make self at home?" the small Chinese man asked.

152

"Nnn .. nnn .. no," Carrie stuttered, completely shaken by the presence of the gun.

With the rifle barrel, he motioned her out into the aisle. "Can explain?" he asked.

Carrie gulped and licked dry lips with a drier tongue. She tried to speak but nothing came out. So she simply nodded. Her captor advanced a step, his sandal-clad foot making no sound, and Carrie backed up a step. Thus, one tortured step at a time, he backed her out of the barn. She blinked in the sunlight and tried to focus her eyes on the white apron he wore over baggy gray clothes. His head was shaved, but when he turned to close the barn door she could see the section in the back. Long coal black hair was braided into a queue which hung to his waist.

"You walk like nice lady. No tricks. Lin Soo shoot you in back easy as front."

Carrie nodded her understanding and turned around, taking care to move slowly. The walk down the path seemed like miles under the blazing sun and perspiration trickled down her back. They came to the fork, one way led to the main house and one to the bunkhouse and mess hall for the hands. She paused.

"Lady know way to big house. Go!"

Puffs of finely powdered dust spun up with each step and her boots were gray by the time they reached the veranda steps. She stomped them off on the grass-covered ground, but it did little good.

"Please, may I take off my boots? They'll track dust into the house."

Now it was Lin Soo's turn to be astonished. "Lady care?"

"Of course the lady cares. The house is spotless. Do you clean it?"

"No, my wife." He eyed her so long through black,

153

unreadable slits she was sure he had uncovered all her secret thoughts and sins and translated them into Chinese. At last, he said, "Move slow. Put boots on step. I watch you very careful."

Carrie didn't remember ever removing boots as slowly as she did now. Though he seemed a gentle man, there was no quiver in the gun. She guessed he would shoot her as promised if she tried any heroics. The time also provided her a chance to regain her poise. If she watched for the opportunity, Carrie could surely convince Lin Soo of her honorable intentions.

Setting the boots neatly on the bottom step, she climbed the remaining steps with unhurried movements and reached for the doorknob.

Before Carrie's hand could touch it, however, the knob turned and the door opened slowly. A petite Oriental woman appeared in the entrance. After Lin Soo spoke to her in Chinese, she stepped aside for Carrie to enter.

With the rifle still in position, Lin Soo presented his wife to Carrie. "My wife, Tama," he said and let his eyes rest a loving moment on the exquisite little person.

Carrie almost laughed aloud at the ludicrous situation, but she swallowed the urge and in her most formal manner, she nodded and said, "How do you do? I am most pleased to meet you. I wish to compliment you on the care you take of Dan's lovely home. I'm sure he, too, must appreciate your efforts."

Lin Soo's eyes narrowed. "What you know about Mr. King?"

"Very little I'm beginning to realize after seeing his ranch. He rode into Parke's Crossing some days ago, badly injured. I happened to be the one who found him."

"He is alive?"

"He was when I last saw him four days ago. Much has happened since then, however, and I don't know where or how he is now."

"He an angry man. Maybe he kill them who take his cows. Then he have to run and hide."

"I don't think so, Lin Soo. There's more afoot than just rustling cattle. Besides, we found the cattle. He wouldn't have to kill to get them back. He could just tell the Army and let them do it."

Lin Soo looked at the rifle he still pointed at Carrie, and back at her. "You not dangerous?"

"I'm not. I've only come here to hide a friend of mine. Her life is in danger and this is the only safe place I could think of. Will you care for her?"

"Your name, please?"

"Carrie Benson." And she went on to tell Lin Soo and Tama about Dan and Alice. Gradually, as she talked, Lin Soo lowered the rifle.

"I fix you bath," Tama said. "You rest, then we eat. Men be in soon for supper. Lin Soo, you must go."

Lin Soo nodded and scurried off down the hall. Carrie heard the back door open and close. Carrie allowed Tama to show her to a lovely room across the hall from where Alice slept, and for the first time since the death of her mother, gave herself over completely to the pampering of someone else. Tama did it expertly.

Chapter 15

After a long nap and a delicious supper of cold roast beef sliced very thin and served with a tangy sauce, tiny, buttered new carrots, hot biscuits, and a dessert of canned peaches and fresh cream, Carrie had to pinch herself to be sure she wasn't dreaming. Tama insisted on serving Carrie in the large dining room at a banquet-sized table. It had been impossible to waken Alice and Carrie felt ridiculous sitting alone in such a room, but Tama would have it no other way.

As she ate, Carrie looked out the dining room window to the pond where the geese she had seen earlier once again rippled the water as they swam in it. A large white trumpeter swan floated in their midst like a queen with her court, and Carrie felt the knots in her shoulders and neck begin to loosen as she let the peaceful scene settle inside her.

Beyond the pond stretched grasslands spotted with ivory-flowered beardtongue. A group of riders on horseback came steadily through the field toward the ranch.

They were led by a lean, broad-shouldered man riding an iron gray quarterhorse. As the cowhands followed him into the corral adjoining the horse barn, Carrie lost sight of them. She wondered what would happen when they discovered the strange horses stabled in the barn. While she waited to find out, she checked once more on Alice.

When she returned to the dining room, Carrie heard a commanding voice from the direction of the kitchen and heavy footfalls advanced toward Carrie. A rugged man, still handsome in his advancing years, bore down on her.

His bearded jaw was set and pale eyes glared from under heavy, dark eyebrows. He shoved the tan Stetson to the back of his head and stood, feet wide apart, his hands resting on his hips. She noticed the flap on his holster hung loose and the hand above it twitched slightly, as though itching for her to try something so he'd have an excuse to shoot her.

What a welcome, she thought and tried to hold the smile she had set to greet the man.

"Good evening," she said, managing a reasonably firm voice. "I'm Carrie Benson from Parke's Crossing."

"So Tama said. That supposed to mean somethin' to me?" he asked in a deep growl. "I never heard of Parke's Crossing."

"I'm not surprised. Unless you travel south into the Wind River Basin, it's not well-known," she replied evenly. Not sure of what Tama might have said, she waited. Until he chose to accept or reject her, there was little she could do.

He squinted and cocked his head to one side. The pause was pregnant with her fears and his suspicions. He was obviously going to make his own assessment of her story.

"Name's Bill. Bill Ramsey," he said at last. "I'm foreman for the owner."

"You mean Dan King?"

"How come you to know him?"

"If you have some time, Mr. Ramsey, you and I need to talk."

"Tama," Bill called, pulling out a chair across the table. When the little woman scuttled into the room, he asked for some coffee and supper. Tama nodded and hurried away.

While Bill ate, Carrie told him of Dan's accident and what they had discovered about the cattle. Gradually the suspicion died from his eyes as she added that the Army thought Dan had been selling whiskey to the Indians and that was why he had left Parke's Crossing.

"Have you seen him since he left?" she asked.

"Not a trace. He's been gone better'n three weeks. We went on a search like he told us, but we didn't come up with nothin'. Thought we'd best get back to takin' care of what was left afore they was all took, too. We been standin' round-the-clock guard since then."

"He hasn't come here then, in the past two or three days?"

"No, ma'am. Ain't seen hide ner hair of him. The boys 'n me, we've been real worried but now I don't mind sayin' it, I'm plumb panicked. Them's some right mean fellas he's a-dealin' with and all by hisself, too. I think it's high time we rode out and see what's a-goin' on."

"Will you ride tonight?" Carrie asked.

"No, but if there ain't some word from him by tomorrow, we're for certain gonna consider a search. I know if we go a-ridin' off and the Army's out there waitin' fer us to do just that, it could mean Dan's death."

"And we can't forget Phil Hardesty and his men," Carrie reminded him. "I think they'd like to see Dan dead, too."

Bill took off his hat and scratched his head. "Sure is a puzzlement, ain't it? I can run men and cattle, but something like this beats me."

He looked helplessly at her. "Sure don't want to do anythin' that might hurt the boss. He's been through enough these past years. He don't need no more grief."

Carrie met his eyes and nodded, but all she said was, "Thanks for trusting me, Bill."

"A woman loves a man as much as you do Dan ain't gonna do nothin' to hurt him."

Carrie's eyes opened wide at Bill's remark. She was speechless. She had said nothing about loving Dan.

"I never said that!" she exclaimed but was unable to hide the blush that betrayed her feelings.

Bill gave her an easy smile. "Some things don't need sayin', ma'am. Just shows, and a body can't help notice. I ain't aimin' to say nothin'. If Dan's too blind to notice, then maybe I'll have to do a little anglin', but until I'm sure, he's on his own."

Carrie knew enough not to try deceiving this worldly-wise man. "I thank you for keeping my secret."

"That's okay." Bill laughed, as he scooted his chair back and stood. "Well, I'd best be gettin' on to the bunkhouse. Boys'll think I took to courtin'."

Carrie chuckled. "That would never do. A man might have to take a lot of ribbing over something as astonishing as that."

Bill grinned. "You got it, ma'am. You got it."

Carrie followed him to the back door. "Besides, I imagine you're already late for the first round of story telling. I understand that's a normal activity after supper."

"They're better called tall tales. Never want to let your neighbor tell a better story than you." He tipped his hat and set it on the almost silver hair.

"If you decide to go ridin', don't be out long after dark.

159

Got some pesky bears with their cubs around after the ripe berries."

How did he know she was too restless to sit? She hadn't planned to ride out, though—not until he mentioned it.

She smiled at him with her eyes and could hear him chuckling all the way down the back steps.

Slowly, she shut the door and turned to lean against it. What a perfect place! She had not only tumbled in love with Dan, but had fallen as rapidly in love with his ranch.

The evening air had begun to cool as Carrie rode away from the barn. The ranch shouldered up to the western foothills and Carrie picked her way across the pasture and up the trail to the ridge of the first hills.

As always, the hills and mountains were deceptive. As one level was reached, another ridge lay a bit higher. Each successive range enticed the rider onward until he became obsessed with the unendingness of them. Carrie felt the pull and tonight it was almost beyond her ability to resist as the far, needle-sharp peaks beckoned her.

Slowly, she rode into the quiet meadow beyond the foot of the first ridge. The sun's last rays shot straight up from behind those beckoning peaks and turned a brilliant vermillion. They colored the clouds and laced the pure blue of the sky, tinting even those in the east until the whole world turned a hazy red from the reflection.

Though Carrie had seen similar sunsets, each new one thrilled her equally, and she praised the Lord for His beautiful gift to seal this day.

Sitting quietly on a fallen log while her horse grazed, Carrie let the peace of evening steal over the land and her.

"Well, guess I'd better be getting back," she said aloud as she stood to mount her horse. Suddenly, though, a branch snapped and all night sounds stopped. Carrie held her pose, not breathing, straining to listen. There it was again. The crack of another branch followed by footsteps. Carrie wanted to run, but something held her frozen to the spot.

She squinted, trying to see through the willows along the stream. Nothing! The unnatural quiet was the only hint now that something was amiss. Slowly, she sat back down. She could be in more danger running than just waiting on the log, secluded from full view of the meadow by the willows.

Upstream the grass swished as though someone or something was walking through it. Bears? She hadn't seen any berry bushes nearby.

The swishing sound stopped. Silence again, then the crickets, one brave insect at a time, joined in until their scratchy chorus was again full volume. Carrie relaxed and settled back once more. Whatever it was had gone; the meadow creatures felt safe again.

"Evening, Carrie." Dan's voice came from behind her.

"Dan!" She pivoted off the log and jumped to her feet. He stood with his hat in his hand, smiling at her.

"Oh, Dan, it's you! I'm so glad to see you! How's your leg? Are you all right?" The questions rolled out of her in nervous relief.

He hobbled to where she stood and sank onto the log, pulling her down beside him. "Had such good nursing, the leg's nearly well."

Dan held her hand, and she made no effort to take it from him.

"I'll believe that when I see it," she said. "It still needs looking after."

"Not that I'm complaining, but is there any special reason you're here at my ranch?"

"Oh, Dan. There's so much to tell you! I found Alice right where you thought she'd be. Washakie arrived in time to help decoy her guards and I couldn't think of any place to take her until I remembered your ranch. I didn't know where else to bring her. She was afraid someone would tell Jed if she went to the reservation with Washakie, and the men who kidnapped her would find her."

"How's she doing?"

"She's scared to death. Found some papers Jed didn't want her to see. She says she was too drunk to read them but he didn't realize that. Phil insisted she was becoming a problem and should be spirited away."

"He and Jed are fine fellows, aren't they?"

"I've been thinking a lot about those papers. They might be the answer to a great many questions. By the way, Phil's the one who told the Army you were selling liquor to the Indians. He even planted a couple of jugs behind the pillows on your bed."

"Guess he decided their trip shouldn't be wasted after they'd been called up to find you. Good man, Phil. Thinks of everything."

They sat in silence, but Carrie drew strength and comfort from his nearness.

"I need to see those papers Alice found." He stood and started to walk away.

"You're not planning to go tonight, surely," Carrie called after him.

"No. Thought I'd get my horse, though. Beats walking to the ranch house."

"You stay here. I'll bring him."

Dan told her where he'd left the animal and Carrie ran across the meadow. It was refreshing to let the wind catch her hair and cool her face. Everything was going to be all right. It had to be for she could feel her life beginning. She had waited so long for this to happen, dreamed it would,

162

given up hope, and then dreamed it again. Dan! She wanted to shout his name to the tree tops and let them bounce it on to the mountain tops. She loved Dan King and from the look in his eyes, she thought he loved her in return.

Breathless, she returned with his horse. He looked up at her and, in the moonlight, the great toll pain and weariness had taken was written on his face. His eyes were red-rimmed and bloodshot and he was pounds thinner than when he'd first ridden into Parke's Crossing.

"Here, let me help you up," she offered as he stood to mount.

Without a word he let her boost him into the saddle. They rode single file up the trail and headed down to the ranch.

At the last rise, Dan paused and looked out over the peaceful scene. "Had a lot of offers to sell. One lately from an agent in Cheyenne who's been annoyingly persistent. But I don't think there's anything on earth would make me give up this place." Looking at Carrie, he said, "I'm glad you're here."

Carrie's heart felt like it would burst from joy as they urged their horses down to the house. The dogs set up a clamor as Carrie and Dan arrived at the back door. Dan reined up and she was there to take some of the weight off his leg when he dismounted. Before he could move up the steps, the crew spilled out of the bunkhouse, quickly assessed his condition and carried him into the kitchen of the main house. Tama and Lin Soo appeared and scurried about preparing a bath and tending Dan's wound.

Carrie stood back as Dan's jubilant men asked questions, trying to catch up on all that had happened. Suddenly, the busy room before her began to spin and she sank slowly to the floor.

Chapter 16

The next morning as they rode south to the Indian agency, Dan kept casting worried glances over his shoulder at Carrie and Alice. Though they had assured him numerous time they were fine, it had no effect. He still fretted that they both should have stayed in bed at the ranch and left the detective work to him.

Alice wasn't quite as vigorous in her insistence of good health, but Carrie, fully recovered from her brief fainting spell of the night before, affirmed with great heartiness that her faint had been brought on simply by too little sleep for too many days and the excitement of recent events.

He seemed to take little stock in her reasoning, however.

"A woman strong as you doesn't faint over a piddling little thing like not enough sleep or nerves."

"Not getting enough sleep for days and living on biscuits and jerky is not piddling. It can wreck the strongest constitution. It certainly wrecked mine."

"There you go! You admitted it! You should be back at the ranch in bed!" he exclaimed, triumphant at having tricked the admission from her.

But Carrie refused to give in. "We've already traveled several miles, and I haven't collapsed yet. Seems like a greater waste of time and energy to go back when we have a four day ride ahead of us!" She knew she was besting him and made no effort to hide her gloating.

"You know, you're a very poor sport when you're winning," Dan said.

Carrie laughed. "I don't deny it. I have a feeling winning when you're around doesn't happen often. I'm going to enjoy it while I can."

"I don't know where you come by *that* conclusion. I haven't won a skirmish with you yet—let alone a battle."

"Want to have a go at chess when we get back to the Crossing? Might be able to redeem yourself."

Dan's eyes widened. "You play chess?"

"I do. Or rather, I did. Haven't found a partner since my father was killed. We don't get many players out this far."

"And I haven't played since Anna died."

Dan's voice, barely a whisper, hung heavy on the still afternoon air.

Carrie was instantly sympathetic. "I'm sorry. I didn't realize she was your chess partner."

"No way you could know," he said. Then he pulled ahead and the three of them rode in silence.

After half a week of hard traveling, they were but a short distance from the agency.

Dan turned to Alice and said, "You'll have to stay out of sight below the hill. It's going to have to be just Carrie and me if we're to find those papers."

"Now, tell us once more what you saw when you were dusting," Carrie said.

Alice tried to describe what she had found on Jed's desk, but she apparently had seen little and rememberd less. It wasn't much to go on. However, a stack of papers as large as Alice described shouldn't be too hard to locate if they were still in Jed's office.

Hesitating a moment, Alice added quickly, "The papers could be anywhere in Jed's office . . . his files . . . the desk . . . his safe." Shutting her eyes briefly, she opened them to look squarely in Carrie's eyes. "I've never gone through Jed's things on purpose," she said, "but I want you to. Please. It's the only way I can help Jed now."

Compassion filled Carrie's eyes as she nodded at Alice, acknowledging both the permission and the anguish in it.

It was late afternoon when they left Alice behind the rise, topped the small rolling hill, and rode down into the agency wagon yard.

Carrie looked at the ground. "There hasn't been anyone here for days. Has Jed shut down the agency?" she wondered aloud.

"I think Washakie told the Indians to stay away for awhile. He doesn't want to start a war he can't possibly win. He's no fool. Or maybe he is—still trusting us after all the betrayal and abuse he's been subjected to."

"He is a fine man, a man who looks at the individual rather than the color of his skin," Carrie said.

Dan reined his horse to a stop and sat looking at the agency. "Got any ideas about how to proceed?"

"No," she said. "I was hoping you had a plan."

He shook his head. "Guess we'll have to take it as it comes."

He urged his horse up to the rail and swung out of the saddle. He reached up a hand to help Carrie, but she smiled and slid to the ground.

"Getting terribly independent, aren't you?" he teased.

"I've had to learn. You're not around a good deal of the time and I can't sit atop a horse waiting." Carrie smiled and tossed her head coquettishly. "You can tie my paint to the rail if you'd like, though."

She handed him the reins and dusted herself off. Tucking in a few loose strands of hair, she let her Stetson fall to her back.

"Ready?" Dan asked.

Carrie took a deep breath. "Ready as I'll ever be. Not having set out in life to be a detective, I'm not sure exactly how to proceed. Haven't even read much on the subject."

"You're doing admirably. Just keep chatting easily and friendly-like. Can't look too serious about a visit to Alice. She's surely returned by now, don't you think?"

Carrie watched Dan rap vigorously on the door. Small tingles of apprehension stirred through her as they waited.

"Doesn't appear Jed's home. Not staying around much lately, is he? Wonder how he's conducting Indian affairs?" Dan observed drily and knocked again.

"Seems to take two firm tries to get that housekeeper to come to the door," Carrie said.

At last they heard the familiar shuffling that announced Matwanda was on the way. Upon opening the door a crack, she gave an exaggerated sigh. "She ain't come back. Don't think she's comin' back. Go away!"

The old woman started to shut the door but Carrie slipped her boot in the crack and the door crunched against it.

167

Dan took the pressure from Carrie's foot by grasping the door and pushing it against the determined shoving from Matwanda.

"You're being extremely unsociable. I'm sure Jed would want you to invite us in. It's been a hot, dusty trip, and we'd like a glass of water."

Making Dan work for every inch, Matwanda grudgingly permitted him to open the door. However, she still blocked the entrance.

"Mister's not here. Don't want strangers in the house."

"Why, Matwanda," Carrie said in her sweetest voice, "we're not strangers. I've been here lots of times." She moved directly in front of the old woman.

"How is it possible that Alice hasn't returned? Aren't you worried?"

Matwanda remained rooted and silent. Carrie backed away, trying to think of a way to get past without using force and perhaps alerting the protective old woman to the real purpose of their visit.

"I need to see Jed about some business," Dan said in a brisk voice.

"He ain't here," she repeated, her arms folded, her face stoic.

"When do you expect him back?" Dan persisted.

"Don't know. He never tells me nothin'. 'Specks me to stay here day after day alone and don't tell me nothin'."

Ah ha, thought Carrie, *an opening.*

"That surely isn't thoughtful. How would you like to come back to the Crossing for the night? Take a break, stay at the hotel, and let somebody else wait on you for a change? Land knows you've done your share."

"Don't have no money. He ain't even come back to pay me."

"Oh, that's no problem. You could be my guest."

Matwanda's face became transformed. Life flowed into it and her tired eyes began to show just a hint of sparkle.

"You'd do that for me?" she asked in a querulous voice.

Suddenly Carrie felt terribly guilty. When she stopped to think about Matwanda's life, she realized it couldn't be very joyful. And there appeared to be little hope of it getting better.

"Yes, Matwanda, I'd do that for you," Carrie said sincerely. She stepped forward and Matwanda allowed her to pass.

"I'll help you get ready to go. We can use Alice's buggy."

Then, turning, she said to Dan, "Why don't you ride on ahead and alert Elsa that I'm bringing in a very special guest."

"I'll sure do that. Take your time and don't drive too fast. Elsa will have a room and supper ready when you get there."

He hurried down the steps as fast as his limp would allow. He wasted no time in leaving, waving good-bye as he pushed his horse into a canter and topped the rise.

Carrie closed the front door and guided Matwanda to her back bedroom where they took considerable time deciding what Matwanda should pack. Leaving the old soul to put her things in a worn carpet bag, Carrie strolled to the barn to harness the horse to the buggy. It was about an hour before dark when Carrie pulled around to the front steps and went inside to gather Matwanda and her things into the buggy.

Not finding the housekeeper or her bags in the front hall, Carrie called, "Matwanda, are you ready?" There was no answer. "Matwanda, where are you?"

In the back of the house the floor boards creaked. Carrie hurried down the hall to Matwanda's bedroom. There she sat, slowly rocking in a large oak rocker. Her arms were locked across her chest and a large Bible lay open across her lap.

"Matwanda?" Carrie stood uncertainly in the doorway. "Are you ready?"

The old lady set her jaw. "Ain't goin'."

Stunned, Carrie leaned against the door jamb. "Why not? Is it something I've done?"

"Nope. Somethin' I 'bout done."

Matwanda would have her say in her own good time. Carrie knew it would do no good to rush her, so she waited, studying the evenness of the braiding in the rag rug covering the pine floor.

"I got sins enough to answer for," Matwanda finally said. "Don't need to go out o' my way to collect 'em. I bin given a stewardship to tend. I promised I'd to it. Lord knows it ain't easy bein' here alone night and day, week in and week out, but He never promised it'd be easy."

She paused and rocked awhile as though gathering steam to go on.

"Promised Miss Alice and Mister Jed I'd take care of the place. Last words Mister Jed give me was 'don't leave the place. I'm countin' on you to keep it safe.' " Matwanda sniffed and shoved her hand into a deep apron pocket for a handkerchief.

"Nope. I can't go. I sure do appreciate your thoughtfulness in understandin' how lonesome it can get. But I got my stewardship and I gotta take care of it. I don't want to be put out like that there feller in the Bible was for bein' an unjust steward. I like it here."

Until this moment Carrie had never cared for the old woman. But she was suddenly moved by her fierce loyalty.

170

Alice must also have felt this devotion. Perhaps that was why she put up with so much from Matwanda.

"Would you like me to stay the night and keep you company?" Carrie heard herself say.

Matwanda's face brightened. "You'd do that for me? After I turned down your offer in town?"

"If you'd like me to."

Matwanda closed the Bible with a slap and set it back on the night stand.

"You put away the horse and buggy and I'll fetch us up some supper."

She gave a couple of vigorous rocks and launched herself out onto the floor at the proper moment, much as a child on a swing would do.

Carrie put away the horses and buggy and trudged back to the house. How on earth would she ever explain this to Dan and Elsa? They'd think she'd lost her good sense, and maybe she had. But Carrie's heart had gone out in understanding to Matwanda. She knew Dan would be worried when she didn't show up in town. And there was always the chance that Jed or Phil would show up. But it was something she'd have to risk. She knew that Dan would come back to check on her. With a quick prayer for his understanding, Carrie knew she had to stay.

Supper was surprisingly good—fried potatoes and onions, beef steak and biscuits. Carrie was starved and it pleased Matwanda to see her eat.

"Never suspect a little thing like you could pack away a meal like that," she said as she beamed over Carrie. "Wisht I had you to cook for all the time."

Carrie wiped her mouth with the cloth napkin and folded it beside her plate.

"I can assure you, I don't ordinarily eat such a quantity, but it's been a few days since I sat at so fine a table."

She stood and began gathering the dishes.

"You go off and occupy yourself. Ain't havin' a guest o' mine doin' dishes," Matwanda said, and snatched the cutlery from Carrie's hand.

There was no need to argue with her, so Carrie strolled out into the hall. Matwanda began singing "This Train Is Bound for Glory" in a cracked but overpowering voice as she picked up the water bucket and set out for the stream which ran through the back yard. If Matwanda had to heat water before starting the dishes, Carrie realized she might have time to investigate the contents of Jed's files. Since it sounded like Matwanda intended to keep singing, Carrie could easily keep track of her whereabouts. Grabbing the feather duster as an excuse, she proceeded to flick dust as she went down the hall.

Carrie decided to leave the office door open, then if Matwanda came to see what she was doing, she could honestly say she was helping out by dusting and straightening a bit.

The room was stuffy from being shut up during the heat of the day. Carrie remembered the oversized rolltop desk Jed had insisted on having freighted in. It, together with file cabinets and a glass-front bookcase, lined the wall opposite the door. A safe squatted in a corner, and framed maps of Wyoming Territory and the Indian reservation hung on the ivory painted walls.

Tucking the duster under her arm, Carrie walked to the desk and sat in the chair. She tried to open the rolltop. It was locked.

What did you expect, Carrie? Think Jed'd leave every-thing out in the open?

The back door slammed and once again Matwanda filled the kitchen with her singing. Carrie could hear the splashing of water as Matwanda poured it into the pan on

172

the stove. Carrie sat back and studied the small keyhole, trying to think of a way to open it. Then it struck her. She had noticed a bunch of keys on Alice's dresser when she had come for her cape.

Humming Matwanda's latest hymn, Carrie dusted her way to Alice's bedroom and through the door. The ring of keys lay where she remembered them. Quickly flipping through them, she found a couple that might work.

Back at the desk, the second key Carrie tried fit the keyhole. With a single turn, she released the lock. Holding her breath, Carrie raised the desk top.

The pigeon holes and various compartments were filled with correspondence and the usual assortment of office supplies, pens, ink bottles, and stationery. With shaking fingers, she leafed through the papers, pulling letters out of opened envelopes. After scanning the contents, she put each piece back in its place. Most were routine communications and acknowledgments from the Bureau of Indian Affairs In Washington.

The desk drawers held more official letters and records. Another of the drawers contained lists of supplies sent to the reservation and signed receipts of their delivery. They weren't recent enough to be of any value, however.

Giving up, Carrie shut and locked the desk. Maybe Alice had only thought she saw something. Perhaps Jed was just angry because she had disturbed the arrangement of his desk. But Carrie's eye caught the safe. *You'd better see if you can open that,* Carrie told herself. *Because if Jed's hiding something, inside's where you're going to find those papers.*

Before trying to hear the tumblers, a trick her father had taught her one long winter's evening over her mother's protestations, Carrie once more dusted her way down the hall. Matwanda, having worn out "Rejoice the Lord is King"

173

began "I'm a Poor Wayfaring Stranger" as she tested the water. She would still be a while.

As Carrie hurried back to the office and knelt in front of the safe, her stomach began to hurt. She had never knowingly trespassed in her life, and the strain caused beads of perspiration to form on her upper lip.

It was a heavy, fireproof vault, but uncomplicated and similar to the one her father had had her practice on.

She spun the knob three full turns to the right, then, placing her ear near the lock, turned it once more until she heard the first set of tumblers fall into place. From there she turned the knob two turns to the left, listening for the combination that operated six tumblers in succession.

After a final twist to the right, Carrie paused to listen once more for Matwanda, then grasped the handle, turned it, and swung open the safe door.

Inside, among other things, lay a large sheaf of papers just like Alice described. The top sheet was a receipt for the purchase of cattle dated within the past two weeks. There wasn't time to go through the papers, so Carrie grabbed the whole stack. Quickly shutting the safe door and spinning the lock, she hurried outside to the barn. There, she stuffed the set of papers into her saddlebag.

Trembling from the strain of her detective work, and feeling slightly guilty, she took a brisk walk. Her thoughts turned to Dan. She knew he would be getting worried about her by now.

Chapter 17

Dan came back, as Carrie knew he would, just before she blew out the lamp to go to bed. He beat on the front door with his fist and shouted, "Carrie! You in there?"

Throwing on one of Alice's robes, Carrie dashed into the hall. She nearly ran into Matwanda carrying a small oil lamp on her way to answer the summons.

"Carrie!" Dan roared again, and pounded the door until the house shook.

Matwanda continued shuffling her way to the door, but Carrie ran impatiently past her and down the hall.

"Dan, it's all right!" she called to him as she struggled with the lock, then flung the door wide.

Dan stormed inside nearly knocking Carrie down. "Why in the name of all that's holy are you still here?" he raged as he stood over her. The thin slice of new moon showed a face pale with anger.

"Have you any idea the anguish you've caused?" he asked, staring deep into her eyes. "Elsa and Alice are fit to be tied!"

Carrie swallowed against the lump forming in her throat. Of course she knew. He had no understanding of her terrible she felt and how hard she had prayed for his forebearance. But at the moment it was useless to do anything but let him pace and rage until he got over his vexation.

At last, Dan paused for breath. "Do you know what I've been saying?" he asked.

Carrie could only nod as tears welled up in her eyes.

At her silence, Dan stopped pacing. Taking the small lamp from the cowering Matwanda, a silent spectator to his tirade, he thrust its tiny flickering light in Carrie's face. Her expression melted the anger in his face.

"I .. I'm ... sorry," he stammered. "I shouldn't have yelled that way."

He stopped talking and, while silence filled the hallway, watched her trying to get her emotions under control. Then, he ran a shaking hand over his face.

"The smoke signals were all around tonight. Looks like Washakie may have lost control of those braves who want every white man's scalp within miles. I ... we kept picturing you in the hands of the renegade bucks out to avenge their starving families."

Again Dan paused, and when he continued his voice shook slightly. "Phil wasn't in town either and I was worried that he might .... " His voice trailed off.

Pain ripped through Carrie at the agony in Dan's voice. It had been a long time since anyone had expressed such concern for her. She tried to speak, but her throat tightened, choking her while the gathered tears spilled one by one down her cheeks.

"Ain't her fault," came Matwanda's harsh old voice from the deep shadows of the hall. "I couldn't leave and she wouldn't let me stay alone."

A few shuffling steps brought Matwanda into the pale circle of light. Glaring at Dan, she said, "If you wanna hit someone, it's me what's at fault."

He looked in confusion at the two women. "I don't want to hit anyone," he said finally. "I just built up such a head of steam worrying on the ride out here, I had to let it go."

Matwanda retrieved her lamp from Dan. "I'll turn you back a bed," she said. "Be just a minute. Give you time to apologize to her."

She took the only light and ambled away, leaving the hall deeply shadowed by the thin moonlight.

Taking advantage of their privacy, Carrie quickly told Dan what she had found.

"Good work," he whispered enthusiastically. "And you said you weren't a detective! I think I'm beginning to guess what's been going on. I'll catch a few winks and then ride out to the canyon where the cattle are."

"What do you want me to do?" Carrie asked.

"I want you to get to the Crossing as soon as it's light enough to be safe." Carrie shivered and Dan reached to shut the door left standing open during the uproar. "And stay there, please. It's been years since I got this riled. My system won't stand too much more." Dan looked deep into her eyes and Carrie saw the shadows of fear—and concern for her—lingering there. Joy at the realization that he cared so deeply mingled with Matwanda's announcement that his bed was ready.

In the morning, after Dan had gone, Carrie did as he'd instructed and returned to Parke's Crossing. She suffered through the day, her mind wandering from her tasks and her eyes trailing from window to window looking for dust plumes on the horizon, the signal Dan might be returning. In the late afternoon, there had been a tell-tale gray cloud in the east, indicating a large cattle herd on the move, but even this disappeared. At last, when it grew too dark to see and still Dan hadn't returned, Carrie hurried upstairs. It was time to insist Alice tell what she knew.

Alice was propped up in bed staring out the window.

"I came to see what you'd like to eat."

Alice turned a vacant stare toward Carrie.

"You've had only nibbles all day."

Turning back to the window, Alice said softly, "I'm not hungry, thank you. I couldn't swallow a thing."

"You want to tell me what's troubling you?" Carrie invited, slipping into the rocker. Alice didn't turn from her vigil at the window; Carrie's offer was greeted with silence.

At last, Alice faced Carrie. "Carrie, my head is pounding unbearably. Please leave me alone."

Carrie stopped rocking and said forcefully, "No! It's past time for secrets. I must know what you're hiding. I found the stack of receipts you told me about. Now I want to know what they mean."

Alice clenched her jaw and set her face even more firmly toward the window.

"It won't work, Alice. I know you read those papers. That's why you had to be sent away. Now, Dan's out there somewhere and his life may be in danger. Tell me what's going on!"

Still Alice resisted.

"Alice, Jed's been deliberately starving the Indians. Did you know? How could you live with it and not try to do something?"

A heavy silence hung around them. Carrie began to

think she would never break down Alice's resolve when a long shuddering sob shattered the stillness.

"Oh, Carrie!" Alice moaned. "When I learned of it, I tried to make him stop. But he told me to mind my own business and stay out of his! I couldn't stand what I saw and I did everything I could think of to help the Indians." She cried even harder.

"Jed and I had always been so close and then about a year ago we started growing apart until I didn't recognize the man I married. Why do you think I drank?" Alice collapsed into soft, moaning sobs.

Carrie slipped onto the bed and put her arms around the suffering woman. "Oh, Alice, I'm so sorry."

"Jed didn't want to send me away, but Phil Hardesty was there when Jed saw me with the receipts for the cattle. Phil called in a couple of his men and they took me. I could tell Jed didn't want them to, but he seemed afraid to try and stop them. I don't know what kind of hold Phil has on Jed . . . ."

"Why didn't you tell the Army or somebody about what you knew?" Carrie asked.

"I love Jed." Alice said simply. "In spite of all he's done, I love him. I couldn't do that to him." Alice dabbed her eyes with a sodden handkerchief. "Now he's gone and I wish I knew where he was . . . and if he was ever coming back!"

Carrie stayed with Alice while she sobbed out her heartbreak and, though the two women said little, they waited through the long night together.

Toward daylight they both dozed, but the first rays of the rising sun struck Carrie directly in the face. Leaving the sleeping Alice, Carrie slipped into her own room to dress.

It was mid-afternoon when Carrie, working at the desk in the hotel lobby, heard the sound of several horses on the street outside. She walked quickly to the doorway. There, in the middle of the street, were six mounted Cavalry troopers and a rangy young lieutenant. Dan and Bill, his foreman, were at his side. Since Dan was obviously not a prisoner, someone or something must have convinced the Army he was innocent of the illegal whiskey trading.

As they all dismounted, only the creak of saddle leather disturbed the silence. Dan, Bill, and the officer handed their reins to one of the troopers who moved on to the stream to water the horses.

Dust layered Dan's range clothes and sleeplessness stained the skin under his eyes and emphasized taut lines in his unshaven face.

With only the briefest of glances toward the hotel, Dan and the lieutenant tramped up the steps to Phil's store. The officer entered while Dan hung back at the door, leaning tall and motionless against the porch railing, his thumbs hooked in his belt. Bill found a spot next to Dan and slouched down. The rest of the troop waited in the street.

Soon Phil and Jed emerged from the dark interior of the store and blinked in the bright sunlight. The lieutenant stood just behind them.

There was a rustle on the stairs behind Carrie and Alice joined her.

"Come on inside," they heard Phil's voice boom, warm and friendly. "You boys look mighty hot and thirsty."

"Appreciate your offer, Phil," the lieutenant said as he picked up the cup hanging on the edge of a bucket at the entrance to the store. "But water'll do just fine."

In silence, he drank deeply, then dipped his handkerchief into the bucket to mop his hot, dusty face. One by one his men followed suit.

Refreshed, the troops quietly stationed themselves around the veranda. Phil's face lost some of its careless joviality and Jed turned ashen.

"Still say you fellas would be a lot happier inside," Phil persisted, his eyes darting warily over the scene as he rested his hand on the revolver holstered on his hip.

The lieutenant walked over to Phil and stuck out his hand. "You want to unbuckle that and hand it over or you want me to do it?"

Phil's eyes narrowed as he stared first at the officer and then around the veranda. Though they rested loosely, every soldier's gun was cocked and ready. He began to slowly unbuckle the holster.

Wordlessly, Phil placed the gun in the lieutenant's outstretched hand. Jed followed his example without being asked, but moved away from Phil as far as the soldiers would permit.

Alice broke from Carrie and ran across the wide street to stand with Jed. She looked magnificent next to her tall, blond husband, the sun spinning red-gold lights in her hair. Jed fumbled for her hand and pulled her tight against him. Alice looked happy for the first time in months.

Wanting to be near Dan, Carrie also walked slowly across the street until she stood at the bottom of the steps leading to the veranda.

"Phil Hardesty, you're hereby under arrest. You want to come peaceably?" the lieutenant asked Phil.

Phil started to object.

"Don't waste your breath, Hardesty," the officer said. "Got witnesses and papers to prove you been rustling cattle, selling whiskey to the Indians, and receiving stolen government property."

"We've been watching you and Jed," Dan said, nodding

to Bill. The loyal ranch foreman straightened and stood shoulder to shoulder with Dan. "Saw you sell your herd to the drovers heading north yesterday. Funny thing, though, it was you, Phil, who pocketed the money. Jed signed the papers, found his horse, and rode out alone."

One of the soldiers stepped behind Phil and bound his hands. Fury glared from Phil's eyes but he remained silent.

"Now, Skyler, you want to tell us your story?" the lieutenant asked.

Jed seemed to shrink until he was a shell of his former self.

The lieutenant waved the sheaf of papers at Jed. "Where's the money for these cattle?"

Glancing desperately at the unrelenting expressions of those around him, Jed nodded in Phil's direction. "Gave it to him."

Shock distorted Alice's features. "Why, Jed? For goodness sake, why?"

Jed drew a shaky breath, dropped her hand, and sank into a nearby chair. The fight was gone from him.

"Phil was my sergeant in the war," he said, rubbing his head wearily. "It was near the end, in '65, and Phil didn't want any rebs alive to go home. He ordered us to shoot the men who had surrendered."

Carrie watched a noticeable shudder run down Dan's back as he and Bill exchanged quick glances. What was going on between the two men?

"I refused," Jed continued, "and Phil turned his gun on me. I ran. Deserted. Later changed my name."

He turned to Alice. "You know the rest."

"But I don't," the lieutenant reminded Jed.

"When we came here, Phil recognized me and threatened to tell about my past unless I cooperated in his crooked scheme to cheat the Indians. I knew I'd be ruined if he did."

"A good try," the officer said, looking skeptical. "But I'm not convinced. You'll have to come along until I can verify your story."

Jed hung his head. "I doubt you'll find anyone who'd admit to being in on something like that."

Dan seemed to hesitate, then stepped forward. "I'll vouch for Jed's story," he said in a tight voice.

A hush dropped over the gathering. All eyes turned to Dan and nobody moved.

"I was there," Dan's words dropped like slivers of ice into the hot silence.

"So was I," said Bill.

Leaning on the railing, his arms folded, the lieutenant said, "Want to tell us about it?"

Unconscious of her actions, Carrie moved up the steps and stood next to Dan.

In a voice so soft heads tilted to hear, Dan began. "Bill and I were two of those southern soldiers Phil ordered shot. We were hunkered down behind some logs and couldn't see his face. Only heard that ugly voice ordering his men to kill us. I've never forgotten the sound of it. Recognized it when I first came to Parke's Crossing; just couldn't place where until now.

"When Jed refused the direct order and fled into the woods, Phil bellowed orders and caused such a ruckus, it caught the attention of a lieutenant. He rode up to find out what was going on. He relieved Phil of his command. Took over and saved our lives."

"Story sounds good to me. Guess after what you've been through, you wouldn't make up a story like that just to save this thief," said the lieutenant. "That the way it happened, Skyler?"

"The first part, yes. Can't say about after I left, but I always wondered why nobody came after me."

Putting one arm around Alice, he went over to shake Dan's hand. "I'll never be able to repay you for this," he said.

"You already have. You saved my life then. I've been in your debt until today. I'd call us even."

Turning to the lieutenant, Dan commented, "I still don't know why my cattle were being rustled at such a rate, though."

All eyes fell on Phil. "I got nothin' to say," he said sullenly.

Jed whirled on him. "Well, I have! Phil took a ride up to see the Yellowstone country and heard what a fine ranch you had. Then he rode by and liked what he saw. Used a Montana agent who worked out of Cheyenne so you wouldn't know directly who was to try to buy it. But you refused all his offers. So he decided that if he could break you, you'd have to sell. Best and quickest way was to steal your cattle. While you were searching for them, you got too close to the holding ground in Lost Canyon. One of the boys spooked your horse. Came back thinking you were dead."

"I'm still going to have to take you in, Skyler," the lieutenant interjected. "Selling government property for your own profit."

"I understand," Jed said.

The whisper of the wind in the cottonwoods, shuffling feet on the veranda, and Alice's quiet sobs were the only sounds that broke the afternoon silence in Parke's Crossing.

Carrie's heart beat in leaden grief. The resolution of the mystery had brought happiness to no one. She wanted to join Alice in easing her grief with tears.

"Did you ever take any of the money?" Dan asked as Jed's hands were being bound.

Jed shook his head.

"Then, seems to me if the money for the sale is recovered from Phil and used to buy cattle for the Indians, Jed should be cleared," Dan said.

The soldiers paused and looked at the lieutenant. He tipped his hat to the back of his head and chewed on his lip. Finally, he said, "Looks that way to me, too," and grinned.

Chapter 18

Carrie thought constantly about Dan as she helped Elsa prepare supper for the unexpectedly large crowd of people. Though he had never said anything specific, he had shown a considerable amount of emotion concerning her welfare. And yet today he had ignored her presence, leaving her standing on the veranda while he and Bill joined the troopers in Phil's trading post.

Her eyes clung to the dining room window as she filled the water glasses, hoping she would see him when he came out of Phil's. Then, Carrie's heart dropped like a granite weight into the pit of her stomach. She saw Dan and Bill come down the street leading their horses. They paused across the street while both men tightened their saddle cinches.

Was Dan going to leave without even saying good-bye? *How could he?* She fought down the urge to race across the street and scream her confusion, anger, and hurt at him. Instead, she walked to the door and stood in the doorway, quietly folding her hands into her skirts as she watched their preparations.

Dan turned his horse until it faced her and placed his foot in the stirrup to mount. When he raised his eyes and saw her, he paused. The lines in his face tightened and his lips grew thin.

Their eyes locked and Carrie felt a pulse beating hard in her throat. She loved this man. Loved him enough to leave Parke's Crossing and go wherever he wanted. However, to be honest, he had never given her any clue that he felt more than gratitude and solicitous concern toward her. She shivered and blamed it on the cooling air.

Dan lowered his foot back to the ground, stretched his arms across the saddle, and buried his head between them.

Carrie drew a shuddering breath and hesitantly walked across the porch and down the steps. She could move no farther, though. She seemed planted in the dust at the foot of the hotel steps.

Dan raised his head and handed the reins to Bill. With reluctant steps, he came slowly across the street to stand in front of Carrie. He tucked his thumbs into his belt and stared at his feet. They waited, neither speaking, until the silence deepened so Carrie could stand it no longer.

"Were you really going to ride away without a word?" she asked, trying to hold her tears in check.

He hunched his shoulders and shuffled his feet in the dust. Little gray clouds swirled up and dropped back onto his boots, leaving a silver patina.

"Surely you don't plan to ride out tonight," she persisted. "And without supper, too." Carrie hated herself for the appeal in her voice.

He looked somewhere beyond her, over her left shoulder, his eyes an opaque blue-black. "We'll stop somewhere up the trail and make camp. We can get a lot of miles behind us before dark."

"You in that big a hurry to get home?"

"Been gone a long time. Ranch doesn't take kindly to that. Men get uneasy. Things fall apart."

His voice held no hint of feeling. If anything, there was a colder edge to it than she'd ever heard.

"Seemed to be doing just fine six days ago." *Carrie, let him go!* her reason said. But her heart wouldn't stop talking.

He rocked slowly on his heels and tipped his hat forward until it hid his eyes. "Thanks for all you did for me. Couldn't have made it without you." He gave her a little salute. "If you're ever up north, be sure to stop in."

Carrie gasped at the dismissal, but could only nod dumbly as he pivoted on his heel in the direction of Bill and the waiting horses.

"Dan!" Carrie called. Words rose unbidden from the center of her being and she had no control over them. "Hear me, please, before you leave. Then you can do as you wish."

He turned around but made no move to come closer. His eyes, glistening black, stared unflinchingly at her from under the brim of his dust-grayed Stetson. His face, though pale, remained unyielding.

Facing this stranger made what Carrie had to say nearly impossible, and she wavered. Never one to leave a task unfinished, however, she gulped down the panic and ran a dry tongue over parched lips.

"I know how the death of your wife and baby must have hurt," she said in a rush. "But I also know you can't live your whole life without love."

Tears pinched at her eyes and her heart seemed to shred with each word. In a trembling whisper, she said, "If you should ever change your mind, be sure to stop again at Benson's Hotel here in Parke's Crossing."

Her chin began quivering and the tears threatened to spill over. She turned and fled into the hotel before he could see more. The receding sound of hoofbeats followed her.

Once in her bedroom the tears burst forth, deep floods that washed over her cheeks and drenched the front of her dress. From the window, she watched him ride away, slumped in his saddle. He didn't look back.

After her parents' death, she had felt a similar numbness mingled with unreleased pain. But then there was nothing she could do to change things. It was different now. Or was it? She had tried and failed to alter the circumstances. She shoved further thoughts deep inside.

Carrie let Elsa serve supper while she sought the familiar refuge of the wide basin and cool, star-studded night. Though it grew late Carrie couldn't bring herself to go inside. Sitting on the back stairs, resting her aching head in the palms of her upturned hands, she stared up the road, wordless prayers filled her heart.

At last, Elsa's voice sliced the night quiet. "You going to spend the night here?"

"Probably," Carrie sighed.

"Won't do any good to sit and moon over that ungrateful man. He's no better than a drifter. Got back what he wanted—his cattle—and he's gone. Forgotten all the kindnesses done him."

Elsa sniffed a righteous sniff. "Knew he was nothing but trouble from the first time I set eyes on him."

Carrie barely listened to Elsa for she knew better. Elsa hadn't seen the ranch, hadn't ridden with Dan, hadn't heard the occasional heart-stopping tenderness in his voice. But there would be no convincing Elsa. At least, not right now.

"You coming?"

Carrie raised dry eyes and tried to focus on the indignant woman wiping her hands on a fresh apron.

"Presently," was all she said.

"Humph," Elsa returned and stomped inside.

Carrie dragged through the next several days trying to feel as little as possible. She dreaded waking up each morning for when the dreams of Dan faded it meant struggling against another day, praying he'd ride across the ford and tie up in front of the hotel. At meal times she helped Elsa and ate only on her insistence, even though she could scarcely swallow.

Each evening Carrie walked into the grove, sat on a rock, and tossed pebbles into the water. Each one vanished without the slightest ripple, the way she apparently had from Dan's mind. She spent the quiet times talking to the Lord, willing herself to surrender her feelings.

Two weeks to the day after Dan's abrupt departure, Carrie sat in the twilight. She picked up another stone and threw it upstream as far as she could. Trying hard not to think, she let the gurgle of the water silence her mind.

Then, a large rock plunged into the creek at her feet, splashing her.

"Oh!" she cried and jumped up, wiping at the water beading on her face and arms. Looking about in the fading light for the culprit, she saw him. Dan was leaning casually against a tree smiling at her.

Their eyes met and spoke for them. For a time they stayed that way, neither saying a word, letting the bond that had grown between them renew itself.

At last, he pushed away from the tree and walked slowly toward her. He picked a blade of grass and, letting it dangle in the corner of his mouth, edged down on the rock beside her. Still in silence, they watched the night sky cloud with stars.

She shivered and he slipped his arm around her shoulders, pulling her to him. For several moments she was content to simply feel his nearness.

"Sorry I caused us both needless grief," he finally said. "Once I get an idea in my head, I have a hard time letting it go. Especially when it involves someone I love."

At the last word, Carrie's eyes fastened on his.

Gripping her hand, Dan continued. "I hope . . . no, pray . . . you'll forgive me for acting like such a donkey. Bill said I was the dumbest—stubbornest—mortal he's ever known, riding away from a woman who loves me. He's refused to speak to me since."

Carrie chuckled softly. "I tend to agree with him. But is that why you're here? Because Bill won't speak to you?"

His eyes opened wide. "You're not going to make this a bit easy for me, are you?"

"No," she said and gave her head a toss. "I intend to extract my full pound of flesh."

"Where did your Christian compassion go? You're supposed to forgive a penitent soul."

"I haven't heard any words of penance," she said, throwing him a wide innocent glance.

Pulling her close to him, Dan wrapped his arms around her.

"I'm as sorry as I can be that I didn't listen to you," he began. "I feel the worst about making you think you meant nothing to me when, in fact, neither your words nor the Lord have given me any rest in the last two weeks."

Releasing her, he knelt at her feet and took both her

hands in his. "I love you, Carrie Benson, and want you for my wife if you'll have me."

The earnestness of his plea marked his face and eyes, and Carrie knew that Dan King had at last buried Anna and their baby, leaving him free to love again.

"Dan, I'd be honored to become your wife—and the mother of your children. I love you—more than I ever thought it possible to love a man."

He stood and drew her to her feet. Removing his hat, he gathered her into his arms.

"I don't know how I thought I could live without you."

Carrie looked deep into his fabulous eyes, now softened and filled with love and she felt she was drowning.

"There's only one thing you must promise me," he said, deadly serious. "When it comes time for a baby, you'll go to Butte where there's a doctor. I couldn't stand the thought of losing you, too."

"If it will give you comfort, of course, I'll go."

His answer was a long, warm kiss to which Carrie responded with all her heart.